NOCENT

OOD

INNOCENT BLOOD

DAVID STUART DAVIES

The
Mystery
Press

To Judy & Johnny,
shining lights in a naughty world.

All characters appearing in this work are fictitious. Any resemblance to real persons, living or dead, is purely coincidental.

Cover photograph © iStoc

First published 2015

The Mystery Press is an in
The Mill, Brimscombe Po
Stroud, Gloucestershire, GI
www.thehistorypress.co.uk

© David Stuart Davies, 20

British Library Cataloguing in Publication Data.
A catalogue record for this book is available from the British Library.

ISBN 978 0 7509 6051 9

Typesetting and origination by The History Press
Printed in Great Britain

PROLOGUE

Autumn 1984

The winding dark ribbon of road stretched out before him, reaching into the blackness beyond the feeble reach of his headlights. The wavering dotted white lines were hypnotic, seeming to merge into one blurry trail, luring him into the dark nothingness beyond. He wanted to stop, pull up by the roadside and just fall asleep. Already his eyelids were heavy and his brain was tired. Anxiously, he ran his finger around his collar. Oh, how he wished he'd not had that pint of beer. Usually he never touched alcohol when driving. It was one of his rules. It was one of the company's rules. And Daisy would go mad with him if she found out. But it had been a long and boring day and the bloody singing competition had overrun, keeping him waiting, waiting, waiting. He'd read his book, scoured the paper from front to back and smoked up. It was only to allay boredom really, he told himself, that he had weakened and had just the one pint. Just the one. To whet his whistle. But now he wished he hadn't. He could still taste the bitterness on his tongue. He was weary and his fatigue was joining forces with the alcohol and the heat of the coach to force his eyelids forever downwards. He kept biting his lip to try and keep himself alert.

The dark, unlit, moorland road over the top from Manchester down into Marsdale undulated and curved erratically and it needed all one's nerve and attention to travel it efficiently … and safely.

Oh, how he wished he hadn't had that pint.

Most of the kiddies were asleep and even the few grown-ups on board seemed to have nodded off. There was no sound from them. He was alone with the drone of the engine, the thrum of the tyres on the tarmac and that damned winding road shimmering elusively out there in the black starless night.

Perhaps he should stop, pull up and step outside to grab a few harsh gulps of moorland air. That would help wake him up. Maybe, but it would wake up the rest of them, too, and make the grown-ups suspicious. Suspicious enough to mention it to his boss. To report him. Maybe some of them had already smelled the beer on his breath.

No, he had to keep going, staring hard, fighting the drowsiness and biting his lip.

The road suddenly dropped sharply downwards and as he kept his uncertain gaze fixed on the darkness before him, his forehead creased into a deep frown as he saw it in the distance. Lying like some giant amorphous white blanket across the road. Less than a hundred yards head, gently seething and writhing, waiting in ambush, was a thick bank of fog. Thin tendrils, curlicues of white, drifted away from the heart of the mass towards him, almost like arms reaching out in an embrace.

He gave a little gasp and, overreacting, braked heavily.

As his foot slammed down on the pedal, there was a high-pitched squeal, like the cry of a child. The whole coach shuddered and began to swing wildly as the tyres locked and slithered on the wet surface of the road. The vehicle had now left his control as though it had a mind of its own. He froze at the wheel as with some awful prescience he knew what was going to happen before it did.

The coach approached the bank of fog at speed, the braking wheels screeching along the tarmac, making the vehicle swerve and shudder violently as though some giant hand had grasped it and was shaking it. Suddenly, the rear end of the coach swung around to the right, colliding with the embankment with a tremendous crunch, forcing the whole vehicle to tip over towards the left. The passengers were flung screaming from their seats as the vehicle was swallowed up by the great maw of white fog. Still travelling at speed, the coach tipped over completely on to its side, sliding and groaning in a shower of sparks across the carriageway towards the drop at the other side. For a split second it teetered there and then with an awful creaking sound, it dropped over the edge and somersaulted downwards into inky gloom. The sound of twisting metal and of the chassis and body being crumpled on impact was mingled with the terrified screams and cries of its young passengers.

Within seconds all was silent. The coach was in darkness and still, apart from one wheel which still spun lazily. The driver, his head protruding through the shattered glass of the windscreen, still stared out at the impenetrable night, but this time with unseeing eyes.

ONE

She looked down at the dead little girl on the slab. Her little girl. The face all battered and bruised and those warm brown eyes staring up at her. They did not see her now. They would never see her again. For a moment she held that thought in simple matter-of-fact terms in her mind, until the full implication of its truth struck her and she shuddered, her stomach crunching into a tight knot. She had no emotion left within her to cry. That would come later. That thought froze her to the marrow. She saw before her years of deep sadness. Empty nights of fruitless longing.

Her baby.

Gone.

Gone before she'd had a chance to taste life.

She was tempted to reach out and touch the face of her daughter but she couldn't. Her body was held immobile by the overwhelming pain of loss.

And then she was conscious of the policewoman by her side. The officer had moved nearer and had placed a tentative hand on her arm. It was, she supposed, meant to be a sympathetic gesture. A practised one, no doubt. How many times had she stood by a mother gazing down at her dead child? Just part of the job. All she really wanted was for her to confirm the identity of the dead body so that she could tick this one off. There were others on her list.

A flicker of anger flamed briefly within her but she didn't have the energy to keep it alight. All her tortured emotions were swamped with an overpowering sense of fatigue. She just wanted to curl up in a ball and float away from the light.

'Yes,' she said softly at length, her voice a flat monotone. 'That's our Debbie.'

Our Debbie. And where was her father? She suddenly had a vision of him as she had last seen him, not an hour ago. He was sitting on the sofa, tie askew, a large tumbler of whisky cradled in his hands and his face red raw with crying. 'I can't go,' he'd said, one hand ruffling the hair at the back of his neck. It was a bleat rather than a statement. 'I just can't see her. Not like that. Not now … not now she's …' He took a gulp of whisky and began sobbing in that strange silent fashion once more.

She had left him there without a word.

They moved around the house like ghosts, neither really taking any notice of the other: not talking, not acknowledging each other's presence. They were dressed in unfamiliar clothes in which they felt both uncomfortable and unnatural. But then, she thought, what was natural about today? What was bloody natural about burying your ten-year-old daughter?

They were both ready an hour before time. An hour before the car was due to pick them up. After a while, once she had checked her appearance yet again in the sitting-room mirror, she sat on the edge of the sofa, ice-frozen, held still and self-contained by grief, while he paced up and down in his ill-fitting dark suit, like a caged animal, his body rippling with frustration, a rich mixture of heartache and anger. More than once his hand reached for the whisky bottle but he pulled back. He must try, for today at least, to refrain. These two individuals who had loved each other once, had been a close couple, had created a beloved child together, no longer recognised these ties. They were worse than strangers now. It was as though they belonged to different dimensions. The bonds had been fraying before the accident, but the loss of their little girl had severed the close links in a savage and irretrievable way. They could hardly bear to be in each other's company now. They treated their sorrow as some kind of dark secret which they must keep to themselves and never, never share.

The rustling of his suit as he paced the floor and the ticking of the clock were the only sounds of normality in that benighted house.

And then another sound. Sharp knocking on the door. She rose from the sofa; he stood still. Neither looked at the other.

'That'll be the car,' he said and walked out into the hall.

She picked up her handbag from the floor and followed him out.

The door opened in the gloomy hallway, allowing a shaft of bright daylight to bleach their haggard features. The driver from the funeral parlour was on the doorstep. He touched his peaked cap. 'Mr and Mrs Hirst?'

The man nodded and gazed beyond the driver to the dark car parked by their gate, the car waiting to take them to the crematorium for the final goodbye.

It was early evening when she parked the car near Scammonden reservoir. The darkening sky was suffused with pink streaks in the west and the ghost of a crescent moon was just visible. Pulling up her coat collar against the cold air, she made her way to the bridge which ran over the motorway. Well before she reached it, she could hear the roar of the traffic from the M62. The air around her vibrated with the sound. The lanes were thick with vehicles now as workers made their trek home. She stared down at the parade of cars and lorries, their bright, beady headlights whizzing past. They looked so fragile, so vulnerable. One little error, one careless manoeuvre and tragedy would triumph. For a few moments she seemed hypnotised by this fast-flowing stream of traffic. It seemed endless. So many different lives on the move, she thought, each with its own joys and woes, secrets and sadnesses zooming by, under the bridge and away to a whole myriad of destinies. Have any of you lost a daughter, she wondered. Have any of you had your child cruelly snatched away from you? Do any of you know that kind of pain? She began crying. It was the first time since she had learned the terrible news. Some inner resolve had held back the tears. She had deemed it selfish. It hadn't been about her: it had been about Debbie. But now was different. This was about her and if she was going to cry at all, it had to be now. She allowed herself that. Her body shook with the release of so much pent-up feeling. Turning her face up to the sky, she emitted a feral moan, like a wolf howling at the moon.

Gradually the tears subsided and a strange serenity claimed her. It was time. Wiping her eyes with her sleeve, to clear her vision, with calm deliberation she clambered on top of the bridge wall. For a moment she teetered there, a gentle smile touching her tear-stained features. She was no longer in pain. She was no longer afraid. The smile broadened as she let herself fall.

TWO

Spring 1985

'Are you sure he's in there?' DS Bob Fellows asked softly.

DI Paul Snow's reply was a curt nod. It was, thought Fellows, typical of his boss, a brief, stoical, no-nonsense response given in a minimal fashion. Snow was not known for his loquaciousness.

'What now?'

'Well, back-up is on the way. I don't think we should waste time. Let's pay a call.'

'Really?'

Snow repeated the nod. 'Come on.'

They crossed the cobbled street and approached the row of terraced houses. These ancient properties had all seen better days but the one with the green door looked particularly worse for wear. The window frames were rotting and the hardboard facing on the door was buckled with age and damp.

Snow knocked hard on it and they waited.

Eventually they heard a sound within. In time the door opened a crack and a man's face peered out. As soon as he saw Snow and Fellows, the man attempted to slam the door shut, but Snow was too quick for him and with force he shouldered it open. With a curse, the man stumbled backwards into the dimly lit hallway. Snow followed him in and saw that he had a weapon in his right hand. It looked like an ordinary carving knife, no doubt snatched up in haste from the kitchen table. With a gruff cry the man lunged forward, with the knife sweeping in a tight arc, but Snow sidestepped the blow. With a snarl of disappointment, the man turned rapidly on his heel to make a run for it but Snow leapt forward and grabbed his shirt collar and hauled him backwards.

'John Andrew Beaumont, I am arresting you …'

The man had turned and aimed the knife at the policeman once more. Snow released his grip and stepped back to avoid the blade again, which this time missed his face by inches.

'Fuck you, copper,' snarled Beaumont, and once more he turned to escape down the hall. Again Snow leapt forward and hauled him back but this time he was not so gentle. Before Beaumont was able to raise the knife, Snow swung him round and thumped him hard in the solar plexus. With a muffled groan, he dropped the knife and his body folded as he slumped to the floor.

'Get the cuffs on him, Bob,' said Snow easily. 'Now, as I was saying, John Andrew Beaumont, I am arresting you on suspicion of the murder of Julia Beaumont and her sister Andrea. Anything you say …'

Later that evening Snow sat with Fellows drinking coffee in his office.

'It's a good feeling to know that Beaumont is locked up, safely stowed away in the cells. Crazy man,' observed Fellows.

Snow peered over the top of his mug. 'No, he's not crazy. Most murderers aren't crazy. They're cunning and angry and driven.'

'What drives 'em, eh?'

'Ah, you'll need a medic to explain that. It's just a barrier that breaks down or a broken fence that tempts you to wander into a prohibited area. Most folk would ignore the broken fence, but some, some are tempted to pass through it. To trespass. It's greed, fury, self-protection or simply pleasure that prompts them to cross the line, but once they've done it, they can't find their way back.'

'Like Beaumont.'

'Like Beaumont. And others …' he said, almost to himself.

'Well, I still say they're crazy.'

Snow gave a deep sigh. 'Yes … I suppose you could be right.'

THREE

He sat quietly, his emotions firmly in check as he turned the pages of the small photograph album. It was a mechanical procedure, one that he had carried out at regular intervals in the past few weeks. It provided him with comfort and a focus, and in a strange way, it gave him thinking time. He desperately needed thinking time. Now that his life was in ruins, he had to decide what to do. The landscape of his existence had been scarred beyond recognition – nothing would be the same again – and he was unsure how he was to survive. Or if he wanted to survive.

He gazed down at the black and white photographs, unmoved now by the memories they evoked. When he had first started looking at the pictures, he had not been able to focus on them because of his tears. But they had dried up. Now there were no tears, no ache in the stomach, just a void. But he was conscious that slowly but surely something was creeping in to fill that void.

It was anger.

He welcomed it and allowed it to build within him, fuelled by whisky, until a plan, a dark and audacious plan, began to form in his mind. He kept running it like a reel of film through his mind over and over again. Each time it started from the beginning, presenting him with more details and greater clarity. The plan was being honed and polished and it was a plan that gave him a purpose again. He knew that it wouldn't give him pleasure, but it would provide him with a kind of satisfaction and a sense of justice.

The first thing he had to do was cut all ties with his past. That was easily done. He thought with an ironic grin that in many ways his past had cut its ties with him. There was only his job that kept him in the real world. He had no family and no strong friendships. He was on leave at present due to his bereavement – his double bereavement – and so it would be an easy task to hand in his resignation. He would tell them he intended to move away, to start afresh where the memories wouldn't haunt him. Then he would disappear.

Once that had been achieved, he could start. He ran the film again in his mind and once again even greater clarity and sharper details were observed. A tight grin settled on his features. It was going to work.

The woodland was still. There was no birdsong and not a leaf, not a blade of grass moved in the late afternoon heat.

'This way,' said Martin, almost dragging Brenda over the crumbling wall that ran around the perimeter of the wood. He was eager and excited and so was she, but there was apprehension and a certain amount of guilt mixed up with her enthusiasm. She was all in favour of the venture but she had never done anything like this before. What was exciting was also rather frightening. Committing adultery was one thing, but having sex outside, in the open air, in a place where anyone could come upon you … well, it might be daring and erotic but it was both dangerous and a bit sordid, too. It had appealed to her when they had discussed it in the pub but now that it was about to happen she was beginning to have second thoughts.

She just wished that Martin had booked them into a hotel somewhere. Clean sheets, a soft bed and, above all, privacy. However, she knew this was impractical. They couldn't go to a place in Huddersfield – that was too dicey – and to travel further afield and pay for a room would take time and cost money. Money that she didn't have and neither did her out-of-work paramour.

'Down here, love. Mind how you go,' Martin beamed, his eyes wide with excitement as he led her down a rough path into a denser part of the wood. It began to grow dark as the foliage thickened above them, creating a gloomy umbrella canopy pierced only occasionally by thin shafts of sunlight. It struck Brenda that he seemed to know the route particularly well. Maybe she wasn't the first girl he'd taken down here. First girl? She almost laughed out loud at that description of herself. Girl? She was pushing forty, had a paunch like a Sumo wrestler and an ungainly lug of a teenage son at home – as well as that other ungainly lug, her bloody husband. No doubt at this very moment he'd be slumped in front of the telly with a few cans of lager on the floor by his chair.

'Not far now,' Martin was saying, virtually pulling her along behind him.

The image of Barry, her lazy slob of a husband, which had flashed into her mind suddenly made everything seem all right. She smiled. 'Good, lover boy,' she said cheerfully. What the hell, she thought, all cares suddenly evaporating, she was damn well going to enjoy herself. When was the last time a man had paid any attention to her, the last time that she'd had sex when the heaving blob on top of her was sober and loving? Time was running out on her life and she was determined to grab what pleasure she could, however furtive, however sordid; however dangerous. Martin was hardly love's young dream with his short, stocky build and boxer's face but there was something about him that she found attractive and somehow endearing. His simplicity and honesty were rare commodities and he was kind to her. That counted for a lot.

At length they emerged into a clearing where thin strands of sunlight dappled the ground. Gazing up, she caught glimpses of blue sky through the tracery of branches. It was decorated at intervals by drifting white clouds. It was quite beautiful and Brenda forgot all her ideas about this venture being sordid. This place was beautiful, romantic, like a Hollywood movie.

Martin let go of her hand and raced ahead of her. Dropping his holdall at the base of a large oak tree, he pulled out a large grey blanket and spread it on the ground. As he did so, he looked up and grinned.

'Come on, girl,' he cried, and sitting down with a bump on the blanket, he beckoned her to join him.

Brenda was to discover that Martin was not a man for foreplay. With him there was no hanging about. There was a job to be done and he was keen to get on with it right away. She had hardly lowered herself on to the blanket before he was fondling her breasts.

'You're an eager boy, aren't you?' she said with mock reproval.

'You know I'm mad about you, Bren,' he replied, his left hand making its way up her skirt.

She smiled and lay back. She was happy to let him have his way with her. At least he was keen and he was a decent enough chap.

She felt his fingers enter her and she couldn't help herself: she gave a little chuckle. When, she thought, had she felt as desired as this? She couldn't honestly remember. Perhaps, never.

Sadly for Brenda it was all over in a matter of minutes. Poor old Martin was too excited. Once he'd achieved his erection, he could barely contain himself. A phrase her mother always used when they were coming back from their summer holidays when Brenda was a child suddenly came to mind: 'Well, it was nice while it lasted,' she'd say with a sigh. And it was. Brenda smiled and thought warm thoughts about Martin. It *was* nice while it lasted.

'Fancy a fag?' he said, struggling back into his trousers.

She shook her head. 'No, I'm fine.' She was glowing and feeling good. She needed no nicotine rush. She gave Martin a kiss on the cheek and clambered to her feet and adjusted her clothing. She felt like dancing, swirling around, kicking up leaves like they did in the old movies. She wasn't stupid enough to think that it was love – but at least it was passion of a sort. That was something she thought she'd seen the last of in her life. She wandered dreamily to the far end of the clearing.

'Careful!' Martin's voice echoed eerily in the stillness. She turned towards him with a frown of puzzlement.

'The ground drops away down there. I don't want you tumbling into the stream at the bottom.'

She grinned. 'OK,' she said, although she wanted to reply that she was quite capable of looking after herself.

Martin was right, though: the ground did fall away sharply and suddenly into a narrow ravine. She gazed down and at the bottom she glimpsed the silver trail of a small meandering stream. In the quiet of the wood, she could hear the gentle rippling of its waters soft on the ear. It was all quite beautiful. It struck her that this serene place would have hardly changed in hundreds of years and yet less than a mile away there was that ferocious clamour and bustle of the twentieth century. 1985 was making its noisy presence felt. At certain sections the sunlight which filtered through the foliage touched the stream, gilding it, transforming it into a bright saffron ribbon. It made Brenda smile.

As her eyes traced the route of the stream, her smile faded and her mouth opened gently. At first she was puzzled and uncertain. Then the cold shaft of apprehension and horror pierced her heart. Gingerly, she took a step forward, her high heels sinking into the soft damp earth, and, screwing up her eyes, peered at one certain section of the stream. She stared hard, frozen to the spot. Surely she was imagining it.

'What are you doing?' Martin had come up behind her and although his query was spoken softly and couched in a pleasant tone, his close proximity shocked her and she stumbled forward, almost losing her balance.

'Whoa, lady, I told you to be careful,' he said, grabbing her arms and pulling her backwards on to slightly firmer ground.

'Martin,' she murmured, a tremble in her voice. 'Down there.' She pointed towards the stream. 'Look.'

'What you on about?'

'Look,' she repeated with some urgency.

He did look and although he said nothing she could tell from his hardened features that he had seen it too.

Eventually Brenda mouthed the thought that was in both their minds.

'Is she dead?'

Martin shook his head rapidly as though to dismiss the matter. 'It's just a bunch of old clothes,' he said, but there was no conviction in his voice.

'It's not,' she said. 'It's … it's a body.'

'Well, even if it is, it's got nothing to do with us.'

Brenda stared at him in shocked disbelief. 'What are you talking about? We can't just leave it there. Ignore it.'

'We can. We must.'

'You can. I can't,' she said. 'They might be alive. I'm going down there.' She moved further to the edge of the slope.

'Don't be so daft. You'll hurt yourself.'

'We've got to go down, Martin.'

He groaned and ran his fingers through his hair. He knew she was right but he didn't want to do it. Whatever the consequences it meant trouble. The police. People would find out. His wife would find out. Find out what he was doing with a woman in the woods. All hell would break loose.

Brenda tugged his arm. 'Look, over there, there's a bit of a track going down. It's steep but I reckon we could make it.'

Martin followed her glance and saw the shiny snail-like path that wound its way through the tufts of yellow grass down to the stream just a few yards from where the body lay.

'I'll go,' he grunted. It was the last thing on earth he wanted to do.

'And I'm coming with you,' she said firmly.

He was about to reply but held his tongue, for he knew that there was no arguing with the silly bitch.

Together they made their way slowly down the muddy path, carefully gauging each foothold. Brenda slipped once and fell on her backside, but she managed to grasp a tuft of grass to stop her slithering all the way to the bottom. Eventually they reached the banks of the little stream without further mishap.

'You OK?' he asked, breathlessly, holding his hand out to help her make the final steps to the water's edge.

With her makeup awry, a sweaty face and a mud-smeared dress she looked and felt far from OK, but she nodded.

As they approached the little figure lying in the stream they could see that it was a young girl. She was dressed in a bright yellow dress – a party dress, thought Brenda – which complemented her blonde curls. She lay immobile, face down in the water.

'My God, she is dead,' said Brenda, stifling a sob.

Martin bent down by the body and with some effort turned it over.

Brenda screamed when she saw the little girl's face. It was covered in blood and her features were disfigured as though she had been badly beaten.

'Oh, my God,' sobbed Brenda. 'The poor thing's been murdered.'

Martin leaned against the wall of the telephone box as he dialled 999. Brenda stood in the doorway, shivering and distraught. The box was dank and smelled of urine and sweat. Felt-tip obscenities decorated the window.

'Emergency, which service?' It was a woman's voice, tinny and remote.

'The police, I want to report …' He paused, his mouth dry and his mind in a whirl. He couldn't believe what he was about to say. 'I want to report … a murder.'

'I'm putting you through,' came the reply – cool, calm and neutral.

'Police. How can I help you?' It was a man this time.

'There's been a murder. A little girl. In Mollicar Woods. She's in the stream. Dead.'

'And what's your name, sir?'

'You don't want my name. You need to get the police to Mollicar Woods. A young girl. About eight or nine. Been killed. Beaten.'

'And who are you, sir?'

Martin was about to slam down the receiver when Brenda moved forward and pressed her body against his. 'You've got to tell them, Martin. They'll only find out and then it'll be the worse for us.'

He hesitated for a moment, his hand hovering over the telephone ready to replace the receiver.

'Go on,' Brenda urged. 'If you don't, I will.'

Martin closed his eyes in despair and placed the receiver to his ear. 'My name is Martin Brook,' he said, his voice flat and unemotional.

FOUR

Paul Snow woke abruptly, his body arched awkwardly under the covers, bathed in sweat. It was the dream again. The nightmare. The same bloody nightmare. Even after a year it came back to taunt him, to unsettle him. To take him to the brink and remind him of his sins. He felt the gun in his hand. He heard the crack as he pulled the trigger and he saw the shock and look of horror on the dying man's face.

But it was Snow, not the dying man, who cried out in agony at what he had done and the cry dragged him back to consciousness. He lay for a few moments staring at the ceiling until his pulse rate had returned to normal. It must have been that conversation he'd had with Bob about murderers being crazy that had stimulated the nightmare again. Well, not so much a nightmare as a reminder of the time when he had killed a man in cold blood to save his own neck.

He lay in the darkness, waiting for his heartbeat to return to normal, which it did after a little while. Accepting that this was all the sleep he was going to get that night – or indeed wanted that night, if it meant returning to these disturbing dreams – Snow sat up in bed, switched on the bedside light and reached for a pack of cigarettes and lighter.

He lay against the pillow, smoking and trying to turn his thoughts away from the nightmare, but the images remained, vibrant and fierce at the forefront of his mind. He heard the gun going off once more, the sound echoing in his head like the shutting of an iron door at the end of a long dark corridor. He grimaced more out of irritation at his own weakness than at the unpleasant memories these sensations provoked.

Stubbing his cigarette out with a heavy sigh, he threw back the covers, got out of bed, slipped on his dressing gown and padded downstairs to the kitchen, where he made himself a cup of strong instant coffee. Holding the warm mug in both hands, he sat in the gloom at the kitchen table as daylight gradually seeped into the room. At length shafts of sunlight formed pools of yellow light on the floor.

It was going to be a nice day.

Weatherwise, at least.

After a second coffee and another cigarette, Snow began to feel more relaxed or at least his old self. He never considered that at any time in his life he was 'relaxed'; his brain was too active to allow for that state of affairs. His mind was never in 'neutral'; there was always something to think about.

And something to worry about.

Living alone, a solitary man, Paul was conscious of all his actions, monitoring his behaviour, his reactions to and treatment of others. It was as though he was constantly standing outside his own body observing himself. He was always on the alert to repress his feelings. Feelings that were not regarded as 'normal'. These were dangerous – as he had found out in the past – and could easily spell the end of the career that he loved. He had to remain firmly in the closet. The poet John Donne had said that no man was an island. Well, thought Paul, I'm out to prove him wrong.

Stubbing out his cigarette, he washed his mug, dried it and placed it back in the cupboard, emptied the ashtray and wiped down the work surface so that the kitchen looked as it did when he had first entered: tidy, and pristine. It was his way. He shaved and showered, washing some of the greyness of the night away, and then got dressed. He took pleasure in putting on a new shirt, enjoying the sensation of the cool material against his shower-warm skin. It was pale blue and he chose a blue and red striped tie to wear with it. He wasn't an extravagant dresser but he took pride in always appearing smart. He was a stickler for tidiness in everything, including dress. Little did he know then that by the end of the day both his shiny black shoes and the turn-ups on his well-cut pin-striped suit would end up caked in mud.

Snow was completing some routine paperwork concerned with the Andrew Beaumont arrest in his office around ten in the morning when Bob Fellows popped his head round his office door. 'Got a missing person … young girl gone AWOL.'

Snow sighed. He had been hoping for something interesting to turn up and take him away from this mundane task, but not that kind of interesting. This was nasty. Missing kids rarely had a happy ending.

'OK,' he said, closing the file on his desk. 'Give me the low-down.'

Bob filled his boss in on the background of the case as they drove out of Huddersfield to the district of Lindley, three miles from the town centre. Gillian, the nine-year-old daughter of Melanie and Carl Bolton, had been reported missing the previous evening. When she hadn't returned home from playing out and it had begun to grow dark, the parents had gone out to search for her, without success. Then they had rung round her schoolfriends but to no avail. Slowly panic had begun to set in and the Boltons contacted the police. The couple had been visited by the village DS who had set up a local search. This too had been fruitless. So far.

The Boltons' house was one of many, all virtually identical, on a newish estate in the Lindley area. It was situated on Buttercup Close, a narrow cul-de-sac where the properties rubbed shoulders with each other and their driveways were scattered with pedal cars and prams and other kiddie stuff. To Snow these houses were the slums of the future. Cheaply constructed hutches with shoddy workmanship masked by superficial glamour which would fade within a year of purchase. Cracks would appear in the plaster, doors would warp, plumbing errors would materialise, the white goods would fail and the cheap all-inclusive carpets would wear thin. Five years down the line they would look worse than a clapped-out row of council houses. These estates depressed Snow more than he could say.

He pressed the doorbell of number 23 and heard the mechanical musical tones of 'Greensleeves' playing in the hallway. The door was opened by a young woman aged somewhere in her late twenties, dressed in a short skirt and flowery top. Mrs Bolton was petite with a pretty face but it was pale and haggard. Her eyes were red with crying and her expression was uncertain, as though she didn't know whether to be angry or sad.

Snow had hardly held up his ID card before she turned away and shouted down the hall, 'Police!' In response a figure emerged from the shadows. This was a skinny young man – the husband no doubt, thought Snow, or partner. You couldn't always be sure they were married these days, even if they had a home and family. The man was dressed in jeans and wore a crumpled T-shirt. His face, unshaven and grey, also showed signs of sleeplessness and distress. He gazed at them, his expression a shifting mixture of hope and fear.

'Any news? Have you got her?' His voice rasped like a rusty hinge.

Snow shook his head. 'I'm sorry, no. I'm here to get a bit more information to help us with our enquiries.' He hated the cold formality of his police-speak.

Without a word, the Boltons shuffled into their sitting room under the impression that Snow and his companion would follow – which they did.

The young couple flopped down on to a battered old sofa and waited. Somewhat awkwardly, Snow and Fellows remained standing. Bob withdrew his notebook and pen in an attempt to appear business-like.

'I know it must be distressing and annoying for you to go over the facts again, but I assure you it is important. It really is a help to us.'

Carl Bolton's face turned sour and he looked as though he was on the verge of saying something angry and abusive, but at the last moment he thought better of it. Snow knew that when tragedy struck ordinary people like the Boltons, they quickly lost touch with not only their own emotions but the usual civilised forms of communication. Their strength and social codes were dissipated by fear and worry.

'What time did your daughter go out to play last evening?'

'It were about half six, after her tea.' It was the mother who spoke. She was calm, her voice a flat monotone. She stared resolutely at her shoes.

'Was she going to meet a friend, a group of pals?'

'We … we don't know.'

'Did she usually?'

'Sometimes she'd meet up with Sally Hardcastle and they'd go on to the waste ground behind the church and lark about.'

'Is that what happened last night?'

Melanie Bolton shook her head. 'No. I checked. I told that copper. Sally had a stomachache and stayed in last night.'

'Did Gillian leave the house on friendly terms? You hadn't been cross with her? Had a row or anything like that?' Bob Fellows asked.

'No, we hadn't. She'd had her tea and was her usual chatty self.'

'And she's never done anything like this before?' asked Snow as gently as he could.

'No, she hasn't,' snapped Carl. 'She's a good girl … a good girl.'

Snow nodded. 'You have a photograph of Gillian?'

'We gave one to that other copper – the uniformed bloke,' snapped Carl, his temper fraying by the second.

'Another, a recent one, would be helpful.'

Melanie Bolton rose quickly from her chair. 'I'll get you one. Anything that will help.' She managed to reach the hallway before the shoulders hunched and the tears came.

As Bob Fellows started up the car, Snow sat in the passenger seat gazing down at the colour snap of Gillian Bolton. She seemed just an ordinary, pleasant-looking nine-year-old with light-coloured hair and freckles. Her smile told the world of her innocence and her excitement with life – that bright future which was in front of her. It would not be difficult to love and care for such a kid and he empathised with the hurt, anguish and despair he knew her parents were experiencing. He was also aware that in cases like this one had to wait until the child was found and usually they were not found alive.

While this dark thought lodged itself in Snow's mind, refusing to budge, a message came through on the radio. The body of a child had been found in Mollicar Woods by a middle-aged couple. It seemed that she answered the description of the missing girl, Gillian Bolton.

'Fuck,' said Snow.

PC Forsdyke saluted as he observed DI Snow approaching through the undergrowth. Snow gave him one of his curt nods of acknowledgement. 'Down there, is she?' he said, pointing to the sharp incline some twenty yards away.

'Yes, sir,' said Forsdyke. 'She was found in the stream. Mr McKinnon is with her now.'

Chris McKinnon was the new bright-as-a-button pathologist, desperate and determined to prove himself, no matter who he upset in the process.

The two men moved to the edge and gazed down. They saw the prematurely grey McKinnon stooping over a small body dressed in a yellow frock.

'Looks like there's no easy way of getting down there,' observed Bob Fellows.

'Or back up. Come on, there's a bit of a path over there,' said Snow wearily.

Slowly the two men staggered and slithered down the banking, their shoes caking with mud as they did so.

At one point Fellows slipped on his backside and shot forward ahead of Snow. 'Shit,' he cried out. 'I'm going to need a bloody new suit after this.'

McKinnon looked up as the two men approached. 'Nice of you to join me, gentlemen,' he said, a slight smile creasing his cheeks as he observed Bob Fellows' dishevelled appearance.

'Not much else that's nice,' said Snow, bending down and peering at the body of the girl. 'What can you tell me?'

'Strangled,' said McKinnon matter-of-factly. 'It's obvious that she struggled during the process as she's been beaten about the face. I'd say she's been dead more than twelve hours. There's latent bruising to arms and legs which suggests she was thrown down here after she was murdered.'

'Murdered ... elsewhere?' Snow said.

'I reckon so. Otherwise he'd have had to carry the lassie through the wood. Look at the difficulty you had getting down here.'

'He?' prompted Fellows.

'Aye, they're always a "he" to me when bairns are involved – until proved otherwise.'

Snow moved closer and let his eyes run over the sorry sight, making a mental image of it for further reference.

She was a fragile creature indeed. The face was badly swollen and spattered with blood, but her features were still recognisable from the photograph he had in his jacket pocket. But Gillian Bolton was not smiling now and never would again.

'Well,' he said, 'I reckon this is our missing youngster all right. Poor kid. Any sign of interference? Sexual activity?'

McKinnon shook his head. 'I think not. The girl's knickers are intact and in place and there's no torn clothing, but I won't know for certain until I've got her on the slab.'

'So the question is, why? What was the motive?'

Bob Fellows moved closer and placed his hand on Snow's shoulder. 'It's like I said the other day. They're all bloody crazy. Murderers. Their mind's all fucked up. What other reason is there for murdering an innocent tot like this?'

Snow did not reply. He couldn't for the moment. Slowly he rose to a standing position and sighed heavily. 'Now we have to go to see the Boltons and tell them their little girl is dead.'

When Melanie Bolton opened the door, Snow could tell immediately that she had guessed the reason for his visit. Her hand flew up to her mouth and she staggered back into the hallway. Snow stepped forward and caught both her arms before she crashed to the floor.

'No,' she wailed. 'Nooo!' It was a cry that Snow would remember in all its heart-breaking, piercing clarity for a long time.

Carl Bolton came running from the sitting room. Initially his stance was aggressive but he soon worked out the situation and grabbed his wife from Snow and hugged her tight.

Snow stood by awkwardly as the two bereft parents hung on to each other as though their close contact would make the truth disappear. The truth that their daughter was dead. It was a fact they had both sensed and realised as though by some spiritual means. Snow had not uttered a word yet about the matter.

Eventually, Carl Bolton turned to Snow, while his wife clung sobbing to his chest. 'How? Where?'

Snow's little rehearsed speech went out of the window. His practised terms of sadness and regret were dumped in the waste bin. He answered the questions in a formal and practical manner. 'Gillian's body was discovered in Mollicar Woods, near Almondbury.'

'Body? Her body? She's been murdered, hasn't she?' The question was barked at him.

'We believe so. Yes.'

'How?'

Snow hesitated.

'How!' roared Carl, his eyes bulging with fury.

'She was strangled.'

A moan escaped from Melanie Bolton.

'Had she … had some bastard interfered with her?' her husband asked, his voice quieter now, more strained.

Snow shook his head. 'Not as far as we can ascertain at the moment.'

Melanie pulled away from her husband, fierce anger mingling with her pain. 'Why? Why would anyone want to kill her? She's just a little girl.'

There was no response that Snow could make which could answer that question or bring comfort to this desperate couple. He remembered Bob Fellows' opinion that all murderers were crazy. It certainly was a convincing viewpoint but Snow believed that even in madness there was a purpose, a reason, however twisted or distorted, that prompted the act of murder. It would be his job to seek out that purpose.

'Can we see her?' asked Carl, his cheeks now damp with tears.

'Yes, of course. We will need a formal identification …' Snow stopped himself adding 'of the body.'

'When? When can we see her?' Melanie Bolton turned her moist, mascara-stained face towards him. Already the eyes were growing empty.

Later that evening Snow and his sergeant had an end-of-the-day drink in the County, the local near police HQ. Seated in the snug in a quiet corner they discussed the case. While Snow had been passing on the sad, bad news to the Boltons, Fellows had been interviewing the couple who had found the girl.

'They have nothing to contribute to the story,' said Fellows, wiping a thin moustache of beer froth from his top lip. 'They saw nothing, heard nothing and know nothing.'

'As per in these cases,' observed Snow dryly.

Fellows gave a sly smile. 'I believe them. Still they've got their own problems. Their illicit nookie session is no longer a big secret. There will be domestic upheavals tonight, you bet.'

Snow couldn't help but smile. 'Don't gloat, Sergeant.'

Fellows' grin broadened. 'You've got to find a little lightness where you can.'

'You've got to find a little lightness where you can.' It was this sentiment that echoed in Snow's brain later that night as he entered Sherwood's, a discreet club for discerning gentlemen in Leeds. On most occasions Snow repressed his homosexual feelings. He had to, or his professional world would crumble. He certainly wasn't a practising gay, but he could not deny his predilection completely. However, he knew that however fleetingly he flirted with the gay world, it had to be done with the utmost care and discretion. He was only too aware that such information would ruin his police career, as it once nearly had. But on occasions he would visit Sherwood's to be with his own kind for a few hours, as an observer rather than as a participant. That would be too dangerous. He was dipping his toe into the pool, as it were, but no more. It helped him relax, to wash away the dirt of his real life of crime and corruption and the unpleasant feeling of denial and deceit about who he really was. There was something that was smooth, refreshing and not at all sordid here. On the surface at least – and in modern society that was probably the most that one could achieve. In his job he had quickly become aware that no matter how bright and shiny the surface, one did not have to scratch too hard before one came to the dirt, the odour of corruption.

In Sherwood's, he would sit quietly on his own and watch, absorbing the atmosphere and the freedom exhibited by the clientele, many like him firmly in the closet for fear of exposure and the terrible consequences that would result.

It had been a wearisome and emotionally draining day. His heart had gone out to the parents of that dead child. With some murders the purpose, the motive, was obvious or at least one could make a good guess at the reason for the killing, but in cases like little Gillian Bolton it remained a puzzle. There wasn't even a sexual motive. Such random killings were impossible to police properly, for apart from a few routine approaches there were no clues to follow. Or so it would seem. All these thoughts drifted through his mind as he sat at a corner table, sipping his glass of lager. He wanted to wipe his mind clear of the day job, to switch off and just relax in an undemanding fashion, but the image of the young strangled girl in the pretty yellow dress, staring sightlessly at the sky as she lay in the stream, kept stealing back into his consciousness.

'You look rather sad,' said a voice in the gloom. 'Would you welcome a little company?'

Paul looked up and saw a tall, good-looking, well-groomed grey-haired man with a tanned face and pearly white teeth. It was the usual kind of coded intro and Snow was used to fending it off.

'I'm waiting for a friend,' he said, as he always did on these occasions.

The man gave a brief smile, flashing his unnaturally white teeth, and raised his shoulders gently in a casual shrug. 'Pity,' he said before melting back into the throng.

Snow admitted to himself that it was indeed a pity, but he could not risk it. As a young policeman he had not been so cautious and that had caused him a lot of trouble in later life. The world was not yet ready for a homo-sexual police officer. Certainly not in the role of detective inspector. To remain secure and safe in the job, he had to behave like a monk when it came to sexual matters. Even his presence in a gay club was perhaps dipping his toe into the waters too far but it was one kind of relief, one kind of release that helped to ease the tensions he suffered because of his hidden sexuality. He denied his natural proclivities to the outside world but he had never tried to deny them to himself. That way madness lies.

He drained his glass of lager. One more for the road, he thought. Better make it non-alcoholic to keep him within the legal limit. He made his way to the bar, sauntering through the crowd, enjoying the freedom to be fully himself. He ordered a tonic water and was about to return to his seat when someone bumped into him, causing his drink to spill over the top of the glass and on to his hands. Men bumping into men in this environment was common and usually not accidental, but Snow, attuned to false behaviour, sensed that this had been a genuine accident.

He was the first to apologise. 'I'm sorry,' he said.

'My fault,' said the man, turning to him, his face suddenly registering surprise, or was it shock. Snow felt that his features must have mirrored those of his assailant.

'My God,' the man said. 'It's DI Snow.' It was clear that he blurted the words out without thinking.

For a moment Snow's mind went blank. He had no idea how to respond to this situation. He had never really thought it would happen. Not only to be spotted and identified by someone in a strange little club miles away from home – but also by a fellow policeman. Indeed, he recognised the man as an officer on the drugs unit in Bradford. He'd encountered him briefly a few years previously. He searched his memory for a name. Colin. Colin Bird.

Now what was he going to say? How was he going to explain his presence in a gay bar in Leeds? Several cover-up explanations immediately suggested themselves to him: he was on a case, following up clues, he'd popped in for a drink not aware of the nature of the establishment, etc. But he knew that none would ring true and all could be checked and found wanting. Then it struck him that Colin Bird's mind must also be racing through a similar set of scenarios.

The two men stood in silence for a little time and then almost farcically they gave each other a grim smile accompanied by a nod and with some awkwardness went their separate ways.

Snow returned to his seat, disturbed and shaken. It was possible that in fact Colin Bird was here on police business. If he was … Snow's blood ran cold. Had his cover really been blown? One thing was for sure, he wouldn't know straight away. It would take the rumour machine a couple of weeks to crank up to full revs. If it was to crank up at all.

All the joy and relaxation had been drained from the evening. One thing was certain now, he could never return to Sherwood's. He cast his gaze around the establishment and left.

For some time he sat in his car, feeling very miserable. He gazed at his features in the rear-view mirror, illuminated by the garish lights of the dashboard. They looked gaunt and vampiric, tinged as they were with a greenish hue. He allowed himself one quietly spoken obscenity. 'Fuck,' he said, with great feeling.

He may not have felt so downhearted if he had known that only a few streets away, Colin Bird stood quietly in a doorway pulling hard on a cigarette, wondering what kind of fallout he could expect from being spotted in a gay club by a respected DI from the Huddersfield force. He too cursed quietly between drags.

FIVE

He was delighted that his handiwork was not only reported in the local paper *The Huddersfield Examiner* but that it had gone beyond even *The Yorkshire Post* and had been covered by the national press as well as featuring on the television news. As it should, of course, he told himself.

He smiled. It was a grim, cheerless smile: one born of heartache and mental instability. It had taken him a little time to come to terms with his mission but now he knew he was doing the right thing. It was his calling. It was the only way that justice could be served. Gradually they would see that. At the end, they would observe the link and then the reason for his actions. It wasn't an easy task. He took no pleasure in carrying it out. But it had to be done. He was certain of that.

The first stage had gone relatively smoothly – if such a word could be applied to what he had to do. It was unfortunate that she had struggled so much and that he had to be far more violent than he had wanted to be. He hadn't expected that. Hitting her around the face to shut her up had shocked him, but he was surprised how some kind of hardened spirit had taken him over and all his usual sensibilities had shrunk away as he became a driven force. He didn't want to be cruel or overly violent. Just a swift, smooth killing was his aim, but when it became tricky, he had tackled the matter in a cold and pragmatic manner. He had to achieve the planned outcome whatever happened, whatever he had to do. That was all that mattered.

As he had gazed at that little body lying face downwards in the stream, he had felt not only a sense of relief, but also the pleasant glow of achievement. Now that he had succeeded once, he knew that he could continue with more confidence.

He pulled his chair up to the single-bar electric fire and rubbed his chin. The beard was making progress. Who would have thought it? He, who had hated the idea of facial hair, who had loved the sensation of warm water softening the skin before the application of a sharp blade in the morning scraping away the stubble to reveal a smooth and shiny chin, would now revel in this shaggy unkempt look. He was beginning to look like a tramp. But then he was no longer the man he had once been. He was dead. Like the others.

This thought brought tears to his eyes and he screwed up his face to expunge them immediately. Practical. Got to be practical. Time to leave this place now. Get the caravan and find some other place to camp out. Somewhere isolated, private and away from here. He looked around the old sitting room. It was really shabby now, not spotless as it had been when Maureen was alive. He hadn't even tried to keep it tidy. Why should he? What would be the point? Yet it still bore some touches of his old life: the family pictures on the sideboard; Debbie's old teddy propped up in the arm chair; her skipping rope and her school coat hanging on the back of the door. He suddenly felt a wave of nostalgia and overwhelming sadness crash down on him. He tolerated its presence for a few moments before hunching his shoulders violently and crying out loud. 'Stop it! I don't need this. It's all bloody sentiment.'

His words echoed around the room. And he felt calm again.

There was no time for sentiment now. Not that kind of sentiment, anyway. He had to be focused, self-contained and determined. Just as he had been with the Bolton girl. He would wait a week, ten days maybe. By then the furore would have died down. Then he would throw more kindling on to the embers.

SIX

Snow re-read the pathology and forensics reports. Although they were detailed, they told him nothing of significance, nothing of relevance to the detection of the culprit that he could not have guessed himself. The most important details were the ones that had been proffered from the start: the girl was strangled and she had not been interfered with sexually. It was most likely that she had been murdered elsewhere and carried to the spot where she had been found. Forensics had discovered traces on her clothes which suggested she had been wrapped in some rough cloth, probably sacking. That was about it. No witnesses had come forward to say they had seen anything suspicious near or in the woods prior to the discovery of the body. And there was no indication as to the motive. It always came down to motive. Cases were much easier to solve if there was an obvious motive, but in this instance there was no clue as to what it could be – if indeed there was one at all. It certainly wasn't sexually inspired. And all the motivations usually involved with adult murders such as revenge, envy, hatred, financial gain and so on could be ruled out when the victim was only nine years old.

'Why this particular little girl?' Snow murmured to himself, before slurping down a mouthful of hot coffee. 'Why her? What was so special about her?'

If he could answer that one, he would be much further down the line with the investigation. It was a question that he found repeating in a much gentler and more circumspect fashion in Carl and Melanie Bolton's sitting room. It was like being in the company of ghosts. They both sat on separate seats, hunched over, pale, gaunt, all the life sucked out of them. They even moved like wraiths in gentle fluid movements as if they were making no impression on the air around them.

Snow had wanted to avoid the cliché line 'I know this is a difficult time for you but …' As he had driven out to their house, he had desperately tried to come up with something more caring, more sympathetic, more original, but he had failed.

'You see,' he said gently, hoping the soft tones would help to ease the crudeness of his enquiry, 'it is a matter of motive. We need to try and find out if there was a reason behind the crime. Maybe someone has a grudge against either of you and saw this as a means … of punishing you.'

'By killing Gillian?' Melanie Bolton asked with some incredulity.

Snow nodded. 'Yes. It has been known.'

'That's sick,' said Carl.

'Whoever killed our Gillian is sick,' snapped Melanie without looking at her husband. Snow was aware that a gulf was already growing between them. He had seen this happen before: the loss of a loved son or daughter bred a kind of guilt which isolated each parent. They both felt responsibility while subconsciously apportioning blame to their partner. It was a symptom of the hurt that they were experiencing.

'Can you think of anything, anyone who might fit that situation? Have there been rows with neighbours or work colleagues? Anything like that?'

'Nothing like that,' murmured Melanie. 'Nothing.'

'Mr Bolton?'

Carl shook his head wearily. 'No.'

'And Gillian was happy at school?'

There was a pause and for the first time since entering the room both parents exchanged glances.

'Gillian was … happy and enjoyed school but she had been a little sad of late.'

'Why was that?' asked Snow as gently as he could, leaning forward in his chair.

'She lost some of her friends in a coach crash. Gillian was a member of the school choir and about six months ago they entered the Northern Championship in Manchester. On the way back the coach crashed and seven out of the twelve kids in the choir along with the driver, the choir mistress Mrs Niven and two parents were killed. It was terrible. Gillian hadn't got over the experience, the loss of her friends. She still had night-mares about the crash.'

'I see.' Snow remembered the incident although he had no direct involvement with the policing of it. There was a terrible dark irony that the youngster had escaped death in the crash, only to fall victim to a vicious killer a few months later. Distressing though this scenario was, it wasn't one that helped him now. There seemed no sense of motive there.

'Isn't it likely that this is some madman? A drugged-up arsehole who likes killing. Gets a fucking kick out of it, out of throttling a young 'un?' Carl Bolton's face rippled with anger and his body shook with emotion. His hands twitched as though he wanted to commit some act of violence to relieve his pent-up frustration. He had addressed this comment to the room, rather than Snow. 'It seems to happen all the time now,' he went on. 'On the telly, in the papers: some twisted bastard playing games with kiddies' lives for the fun of it while they run bloody circles round the police. You never catch the fuckers, do you?'

Snow wasn't about to argue. He knew that it was pain and anger speaking rather than reason. 'We'll try our best to bring to justice the person who took Gillian's life,' he said simply. He was aware how facile and pathetic these words sounded to the two wounded creatures who sat opposite him, but for the time being it was the best he could give them. He certainly wasn't about to promise them that without doubt he would catch their daughter's killer.

With a sigh and a gentle smile, Snow rose and began making his way to the door. He turned and gazed at the couple, each caught and isolated in their own grief. Maybe it was that their daughter had been the only real link that they had with each other: the fragile glue that held a stale marriage together. Now she was gone they had nothing. It was not rare; Snow had seen it before. 'Sorry to have bothered you,' he said, 'but please, if you do think of anything, however slight or apparently insignificant it seems, please let us know. Goodbye for now. I'll let myself out.'

It had played on Miranda's mind for some time and had even stopped her sleeping properly. Now she had come to a decision. She needed to confide in her mum. Instinctively rather than rationally, she knew that in talking to her mother she would release some of the anguish she felt. Initially, she hadn't regarded it as a secret but the longer she had kept it to herself it had grown into one, a dark and unpleasant secret, one that bred a strange sense of guilt within her. She needed to share that guilt, to release it.

When Miranda got back from school, she found her mother, as usual, in the kitchen. She was chopping up some vegetables for their evening meal.

'Hi, hon,' she called over her shoulder. When the little girl did not reply as she usually did, she stopped what she was doing and turned round to face her, and saw the gloomy, tired expression on her daughter's face.

'What is it, baby? You had a bad day?'

These kind words broke the dam and the girl ran to her mother and hugged her, while tears welled up in her eyes.

'What is it, darling? What on earth's the matter?'

'It's Gillian,' sobbed Miranda, snuggling her face into her mother's apron.

'Of course it is.'

Of course it was. Her mother was fully aware that losing a friend at her age was bad enough, but in such a terrible manner it must have eaten away at her little angel. Miranda had been so terribly brave about it, or so it seemed, but she must have been bottling it all up until now. She hugged her daughter tightly as her little body rippled and shook with sobs.

'Let it all out, darling. There's nothing to be ashamed of. You loved Gillian, I know. Just remember she's with the angels now. You can send a message to her in your prayers tonight.'

Suddenly the girl pulled away and turned her red tear-stained face up towards her mother. 'It's not just that. I know something.'

At these words, her mother felt a thin shaft of fear enter her body. 'Something?' she said, as easily as her dry mouth would allow.

Miranda nodded.

Her mother knelt down so that their faces were on a level. 'What do you mean? What do you know? You can tell me.'

Miranda ran her sleeve across her eyes in an attempt to mop up the surplus tears. 'Gill and I had a row and we fell out.'

'What about?'

Miranda's face screwed up again as the tears reappeared. 'I can't remember now. It was so stupid.'

'That's nothing to get upset about. Friends always fall out from time to time. That's because they are so close. Daddy and I fall out sometimes, but we still love each other.'

Miranda shook her head vigorously. 'No, no, that's not it.'

'Well, you tell me what it is, eh?' She leaned forward and planted a kiss on her daughter's forehead.

'We usually came home together but … on that day we had fallen out, Gill set off without me. She was very angry. I wanted to catch up with her but she walked so fast … so fast.'

'Yes.'

'Well, I was following her and then I saw her talking to a man with a van.'

The shaft of fear intensified.

'A man with a van …? What do you mean?'

'He pulled up by the pavement and leaned out of the window to speak to her.'

'What did he say?'

Miranda shook her head. 'I don't know. I was too far away to hear. But then she got into the van.'

'She got … Are you sure about this? Very sure?'

Miranda gave a strong affirmative nod. 'And then they drove off.'

Her mother rose and moved back to lean against the work surface to give herself some support. 'Oh, my God,' she mouthed, the words hardly audible.

'Perhaps he was a bad man. The man that … I'm sorry for not telling you.' Miranda began to cry again.

'That's all right, darling,' said her mother, ruffling her daughter's hair absent-mindedly while her thoughts were in free-fall. 'At least you have done now.' She glanced at the telephone on the wall. She knew that she would have to inform the police.

It was Bob Fellows who took the call when it was passed on to the incident room. Snow was in the kitchen area making a brew. Bob jotted down the information and address and assured Mrs Stone that they'd be over at her house in quick sticks.

'Breakthrough, guv,' he cried as he popped his head around the door. 'That coffee will have to wait.'

SEVEN

'What did this man look like?'

Miranda had now grown shy and awkward. She had hoped that in telling her mum about Gillian and the man with the van, her mum would simply tell the police and that would be the end of it. She hadn't reckoned on the police coming to her house. That really unnerved her. Now here she was on the sofa in her sitting room, facing this strange man with the long narrow face and penetrating eyes, being asked questions. He seemed a nice man. He looked kind of sad and rather too thin, but he was smart in his dark suit and shiny shoes. He had leaned close to her and spoke softly and she could also smell his aftershave. It was sort of bitter-sweet like pear drops.

Snow had turned up at the house alone without his sergeant, thinking that two policemen invading the property might easily spook the young girl. It was clear to him now that his solo appearance had intimidated the girl. He should have brought DS Susan Morgan or a WPC with him maybe, someone who would be more attuned to dealing with youngsters. Despite assuring her in gentle terms that she was not in any trouble, the little girl seemed apprehensive and nervous in his presence.

He repeated his question as mildly as he could: 'What did this man look like?'

'I'm not sure,' Miranda said, biting her top lip nervously. 'I only saw his head poking out of the van.'

'Was he a young man or an old man?'

Miranda shrugged and pursed her lips. 'Oldish, I guess. I saw that he had a bald spot.'

'Did he have dark hair or grey? Or perhaps he was blond like your mummy.'

Instinctively Miranda looked at her mother and then shook her head. 'He wasn't blond. His hair was sort of ordinary. Brownish, I suppose.'

'Did he have a beard or a moustache?'

She paused and screwed up her face in thought. 'I don't think so. I can't be sure. He might have had a beard. I think his chin was sort of dark.' This uncertainty seemed to worry her and she glanced round at her parents for support. Her mother gave her an encouraging smile. 'You're doing fine, angel.'

'Do you think anyone else saw Gillian get in the van?' Snow asked.

'Oh, no. I was the only one on that bit of the street. I had hurried to keep up with her, you see. I was going to try and make friends with her again …' Miranda's voice faltered and her eyes moistened.

Snow touched her arm. 'That's all right, love. Don't fret. What can you tell me about the van? What colour was it?'

'It was brownish.'

'Brownish?'

'Like a biscuit.'

'Light brown.'

Miranda nodded.

'Did it seem old or new?'

'Old, I think. It looked dirty and a bit rusty.'

'Do you remember any of the numbers on the number plate?'

Miranda shook her head.

'Or the make?'

Another shake of the head.

He knew these questions about the van were crucial. He might have had more luck if his witness had been a little boy, for they tended to be interested in vehicles. A lad might have noted more details about it, including the registration number, but girls were observant in different ways.

'If I showed you pictures of some vans, do you think you could pick out the one you saw?'

After a moment's thought, she nodded. 'I think so,' she said quietly.

'Is there anything else that you remember about the man or the van …?'

The girl thought for a moment and then it looked like she was about to shake her head when she stopped. 'Yes,' she said slowly. 'There was something. There was a sticker on the back window. Like a flag. A triangular flag. It was bright red with white or cream letters.'

'Letters … what did they say?'

'It was something about Blackpool, I think. Yes, I think there was a drawing of Blackpool Tower on it.'

Snow smiled and patted her arm. 'Well, thank you, Miranda. You've been brilliant,' he said and rose to his feet.

He was about to move away to address the parents when the little girl grabbed his sleeve. 'You will catch him, won't you?' she asked. 'You will catch that man who killed my friend?'

It was late when Snow got back to the office. It was empty apart from Bob Fellows.

'They've gone to the County. To celebrate Sue's birthday,' he said, slipping on his mac. 'They're expecting you to pop in.'

Snow nodded wearily. This was the last thing he wanted. He was tired and he never felt comfortable in the social setting with his fellow officers. He reckoned he hadn't the facility to switch off being their boss and convert into one of their mates. Hierarchies can't function like that without something being lost. Respect? Allegiance? Discipline? He knew he was a prig about this but it was innate not learned and as such pretty well immutable. And for Snow small talk was a foreign language.

'I'll walk across with you,' he said.

As they strolled along Market Street and down Princess Street to the County, Snow filled in his sergeant with the details of his interview with Miranda Stone. 'So, we need to get a set of pictures of small vans manufactured within the last ten years and see if she can pick one out for us.'

Bob nodded but did not comment. Both men knew that even if the girl could spot the exact model they were still in the 'needle-in-a-haystack' territory.

The County was an old-fashioned town pub. The décor hadn't changed much since the fifties. It was full of mirrors, old leather-type seats, brass ornaments that could have done with a polish, and framed pictures of country scenes, all wreathed in a thick fug of cigarette smoke. As they entered, they could hear the jovial chatter from the small room at the back of the pub where the police officers had gathered.

'They sound merry,' observed Snow.

'They've been here over an hour.'

'A pint?'

'Thanks, sir. I'll have Tetley's.'

Snow ordered and then they took their foaming pints into the small room. The fuggy, noisy atmosphere embraced them as they entered.

'Cheers, sir,' cried out PC Woodcock in greeting. He was a lanky, still-wet-behind-the-ears youngster who hadn't quite mastered the niceties of dealing with superior officers. Others in the group gave more sedate nods and muttered respectful welcomes. The unwritten rule in the culture was never get too pally with those in ranks above you.

'Where is the birthday girl?' said Snow, acting out his part as the jovial boss.

'I'm here, sir.' The voice came from behind him and he turned and saw DS Susan Morgan. She wore a paper hat and a rather woozy grin. 'Glad you could make it.'

Snow raised his glass. 'Happy birthday, love.' He clinked her glass. He was fond of Susan. She was a sensible, no-nonsense police officer and thoroughly reliable. Although at the moment she looked as though she was on the way to being inebriated.

'Come and sit down, sir,' she said, patting the space on the bench by her.

Snow obliged and this was a signal for the various conversations and raucous noise to resume.

'I'm not sure that when you get to my age you should celebrate birthdays,' she said, staring down into her drink.

Snow laughed. 'You talk as though you're ancient. You're a young woman yet. Don't forget it.'

She smiled a dreamy smile at him. 'Really. Do you think so?'

Snow gazed at her. She was a pretty woman in her mid-thirties. She'd had a difficult private life, including a nasty divorce, the stress and strain of which still showed in her features even in repose. She lived alone and her whole existence, it seemed to Snow, was now focused on her police work. Not unlike himself in many respects.

'You got any plans for your birthday?' he asked. He knew he was beginning to struggle already. He had wandered into the mire of small talk.

'Apart from getting blathered in here, you mean?' She giggled.

'Yes,' he said, grinning despite himself, 'apart from that.'

She shook her head. 'No. Just an early night in preparation for the hangover in the morning.' She smiled again but the eyes were sad.

Snow made no response, simply because he couldn't think of one.

'It gets sort of lonely at times, doesn't it? I mean you're a bit like me … in the sense that you've no family, no partner, just an empty place to go back to.'

It was a theme that Susan had touched on before with Snow. He knew she was right but he really didn't want to go down that particular avenue.

He grinned and raised his hand. 'You've a room full of friends, all happy for you.'

Susan gave him a strange look. Suddenly she seemed very sober and astute. 'A room full of friends,' she repeated flatly. 'A room full of friends.'

They both gazed around at the assembled throng, each chatting, drinking, smiling, each absorbed in their own little cocoon.

Susan raised an eyebrow and Snow knew exactly what she meant.

EIGHT

A week passed without any real progress or development in the investigation of the murder of Gillian Bolton. This was the usual rhythm of a murder case, unless something sensational turned up. And nothing sensational had turned up. So after the initial flurry of activity came the depressing lull. The case was flatlining. Snow was used to it, but that did not mean that it made it any the less frustrating. It all added to his sense of impotence and incompetence. He was aware that the parents of the little girl and the general public who were following the case would see the police as lacking or slacking. Clueless and incompetent. Yet another unsolved crime.

Miranda had identified the kind of van she thought her friend had got into, but both Snow and Bob Fellows could tell from the girl's demeanour and the nervous flicker of her eyes as she pointed it out that she was not really sure. It was an educated guess at best. She wanted to please them and her parents and more than anything to have done with the matter. However, a call had gone out to check on a fawn-coloured Ford Cavalier, registered in the area within the last ten years. It was a faint hope but at least it was a hope.

Snow had also to deal with a wodge of paperwork on the Andrew Beaumont case. This, he thought wryly, kept him out of mischief. After seven days, the girl's murder had disappeared from the newspapers, even the local one, and there was no mention in the television bulletins any more. Well, it simply was no longer important. Not to them, anyway.

'They're just waiting for an arrest … or another victim,' observed Bob Fellows.

'Don't,' said Snow, knowing all too well that his sergeant was right.

Later that day, Snow, as usual, was the last to leave the office, or so he thought. He was just about to turn the lights off when DS Susan Morgan wandered out of the little kitchen area.

'Still here,' he said automatically, immediately aware that it was a stupid redundant observation and he regretted making it.

Susan nodded. 'I was waiting to have a word.'

'Oh?'

She glanced down, examining her fingernails. 'About the other night. In the pub. I hope … I hope I wasn't too familiar.'

Snow gave her one of his crooked little grins. 'You were a little squiffy. But you were allowed. It was your birthday, after all.'

'Maybe. You see … I was trying to pluck up courage. The drink was going to give me the nerve. But it didn't quite work. It gave me cold feet instead.'

Snow had an awful premonition where this was going, but he remained silent and still.

'I've been meaning to do it for ages.' She grinned shyly and took a deep breath. 'You see, I really like you and I reckon we're paddling in similar canoes: single and rather lonely …'

He meant to stop her there but he couldn't. He couldn't be so brutal.

'I was going to ask you out,' she said boldly. She was looking at him now, her blue eyes focusing on his face. 'On a date,' she added as an afterthought, as though she hadn't made herself clear. She sighed and bit her lip. 'There … I've said it.' She paused a moment, waiting for Snow to respond, but he didn't so she carried on: 'It doesn't always have to be the bloke that does the asking. I mean we live in a society where there are equal rights …' She chuckled nervously.

Snow found himself lost for words. His mind searched for the most appropriate response to this unexpected situation but without much success. He liked Susan and enjoyed her company but of course a romance or any kind of relationship was out of the question. He knew he had to let her down as gently as possible while at the same time giving no hints or suggestions as to his real sexual orientation. That last phrase seemed so pompous and silly to him at this particular moment. He knew how hurtful rejection could be and in this case it had nothing to do with how he felt about Susan. He liked her. He was fond of her. He had no desire to hurt her. It was just, to use her imagery, that his canoe was paddling in the opposite direction. He opened his mouth to speak but nothing came out.

In the end it was Susan herself who came to his rescue. 'I've embarrassed you. I'm sorry. Perhaps it was a bad idea,' she said, sensing Snow's reluctance.

A lifeline! And Snow grabbed it. 'No, no, it's not that, but you know relationships in the same team are frowned on – discouraged.' It was a little lame but it would have to do. He still felt cruel and unfeeling saying it.

'Especially between a Detective Inspector and a lowly DS, eh?' Susan gave him a half-hearted smile and took a step back.

Snow knew it couldn't end like this. Some reparation was necessary. He moved forward and touched her arm. 'Rank really has nothing to do with it. Believe me. But life would get very tangled if … Well, you know what I mean. I'm sorry. It would be nice … under different circumstances. I guess I'm married to the job. Anyway … to be honest I reckon I'm not good enough for you.' He leaned close and kissed her gently on the cheek. 'You deserve someone better.'

He knew the words were crass; he just hoped that the gesture would be understood and accepted.

'Someone better,' she repeated softly, her eyes tearing up now. She turned quickly and headed for the door. Snow caught the words 'Goodnight, sir,' before the door swung shut.

Snow emitted an inarticulate groan as he slammed his fist down on the desk. Why was life so bloody difficult?

NINE

That was another one over. Thank heavens. Urgh! How she hated them. Those horrible piano lessons. Her mum and dad were monsters, forcing her to go on with this torture when she had told them just how much she hated having to go to Mrs Perkins for an hour every week for the rotten lessons. It was torture. She had begged them to let her give up. But no. They would not budge. She had tried to convince them that she really had no talent for playing the piano but still they wouldn't listen. She wasn't getting any better either. She knew it. In fact she was getting worse. It took her all her time to concentrate while Mrs Perkins harped on about 'straight back' and 'spread your fingers, Angela'. Dreary old bag. And she smelt too. Her mum said it was lavender water but Angela thought it was wee. The old bag must be nearly a hundred. She had thin wispy grey hair that she wound around her head in a weird and complicated fashion and held in place with a leather brooch-like contraption at the back. Despite all the powder she plonked on her face, she couldn't hide all those lines that crisscrossed her ancient phizzog. And another thing: she had never seen a Mr Perkins. He could be dead, of course. Or run away to get away from that strange hair, white crinkled face and the smell of wee, but Angela reckoned there had never been a Mr Perkins. No one would want to marry the silly, smelly old thing. She had made the Mrs bit up just to appear normal and respectable.

As Angela shut the front door of Mrs Perkins' cottage, she gave a sigh of relief. At least it would be another seven days before she would have to return. Of course, there were the practice sessions at home but at least she was on her own then. If only her mum and dad would let her concentrate on her singing. That's what she liked best and she knew that's what she did the best as well.

She walked down to the end of the street, the spring evening already fading. She'd get home and watch a bit of telly and then it would be time for bed.

'Excuse me. I'm looking for Bradley Street,' said a voice close to her.

She turned and found herself facing a tall, rather dishevelled man, wearing a long raincoat and a scruffy flat cap. In one hand he held a sheet of paper.

'Do you know where this is?' he asked, moving nearer and holding out the sheet of paper.

Angela could see there was an address on the paper but it was written in pencil, in wild indecipherable handwriting. She peered closer. As she did so, the man suddenly clamped his other hand around her mouth. He had a pad in it. It smelt funny and strong, like disinfectant. The fumes filled her mouth and nose and soon began to affect her vision and then her brain. She struggled at first, her legs kicking wildly, but then she seemed to lose all her energy. She felt very weak and all the sounds started to fade as though she was going deaf, and it grew very dark. Within seconds she had blacked out.

The man scooped her up and hauled her body into the back of a van that was parked by the kerb. There was no one else about.

Inside the van, the man secured the girl's hands and legs with some rope and taped over her mouth. With a satisfied smile, he clambered out, slammed the rear door shut and locked it. Within seconds he was in the driving seat and turning the ignition. He was hugely satisfied. It had all gone like clockwork.

It wasn't long before the smile had disappeared from his lips. The clever part of the operation was over. Now came the really hard bit. He wasn't a violent man by nature. Circumstances had made him one. It was just that he had to stoke himself up like some kind of fiery boiler in readiness for the final act. He had to remember the pain, the anguish and the fury. As he drove, he conjured up images in his mind to reassure himself that he was doing the right thing, that he *could* do the right thing, that he *would* do the right thing.

Within twenty minutes he had reached the chosen spot, a woodland area accessed down a steep path on Heaton Road. He pulled the van off the road into a little copse and turned his headlights off. He sat patiently, waiting for it to fall fully dark. When he was ready, he climbed over the driver's seat into the back of the van and gazed at the young girl lying there. He hesitated for a fraction but he knew he had to act before she woke up. He didn't want a repeat of the tussle he'd had last time. It would be better for her too.

He leaned forward and clamped his hands around her throat. He applied pressure, gently at first and then harder. The girl stirred and a strange rasping noise emanated from the tape covering her mouth. Briefly, her unseeing eyes opened and seemed to stare accusingly at him. He turned away but tightened his grip on the girl's neck. The feel of the smooth, supple and vulnerable skin gave him strength. Now he could do it. Now, he almost enjoyed it. Her body stirred gently at first and then she squirmed more vigorously in her death throes, as though experiencing a bad dream. His fingers tightened even more. He could feel her windpipe crushing under the force. She emitted a muffled cry and then with a final shudder, the girl lay still.

He fell back against the inner wall of the van, his eyes filled with tears and his chest heaving with sobs.

Sometime later, having wrapped the girl's body in a large sheet of rough sacking, he carried it down through the woods towards the large pool that lay at the bottom of the slope. The water lay still and black like treacle under the darkened sky. He struggled on to the short wooden jetty used by anglers. He took the body out of its wrapping and, with as much effort as he could muster, he hurled it into the pool. There was a gentle splash and initially it disappeared from sight, but then with grim inevitability it slowly returned to the surface, a white elbow just breaking the surface of the scummy water.

He wrapped up the sacking and with one final look at the body floating just beneath the surface of the pool, he made his way up the slippery path back to the van. He was neither elated nor sad. He felt numb. But he was conscious that his job was not yet half done.

TEN

'Certainly looks like the same fellow – if a fellow it be, as you might say,' observed Chris McKinnon, as he rose from his crouching position to face Paul Snow.

'Strangled?'

McKinnon nodded. 'Virtually identical to the other one. But no bruises around the face this time. He's getting better with practice.'

Snow gave the pathologist a withering glance. He knew this gallows-type humour was typical of the breed and in many ways helped them to cope with the ghoulish nature of their profession, but it did effectively remove any sympathetic concern for the victim and that was too harsh for Snow's sensibilities. He gazed down at the corpse of the young girl and felt infinitely sad.

'If you're right,' Snow said at length, 'it's likely that we have a serial killer on our hands – and those bastards prove to be not only cunning but barmy too: a devilish combination. Logical, practical policing is useless when you get one of those weird sods rampaging about the countryside killing young kids.'

McKinnon wanted to say, 'Not my problem', but he had enough sense to gauge Snow's mood and hold the comment back. It might be a smart riposte, and indeed true, but it wouldn't help his relationship with Snow. Instead he resorted to a weary shrug.

Bob Fellows joined them at the waterside. 'Just had a call from HQ,' he said. 'A young girl matching this one's appearance went missing last night. Angela Cleeves. She never returned home from her music lesson.'

'Better get DS Morgan to go and see the parents. Get a photo of the lass. No point in putting them through an identification procedure until we're fairly certain. If this is Angela, then we'll need the usual background material. Could you follow that up in due course, Bob?'

Fellows gave a mock salute. 'Righto, sir.' He then cast a glance down at the mud-stained body which lay just a few feet away. 'A pretty lass.'

'Yes,' said Snow. 'She was.'

It transpired, as Snow had expected, that the corpse that had been found floating in the pond in Heaton woods was indeed that of Angela Cleeves. Bob had arranged for the parents to identify the body formally and to gather what detail he could about the girl and in particular her movements the previous evening. Snow had gone through this harrowing procedure with the Boltons and he was determined to give this one a miss. He knew he was a coward, avoiding being there when Angela's mother and father saw their daughter for the last time, when the white sheet was pulled back to reveal the stark, pallid face of their little girl, her glassy eyes staring into space, the hair scraped back and the livid, dark bruises all around her neck. It would break the heart of the sternest of men and he was far from that. He had no desire for children himself, but he empathised with anyone who lost one in such cruel circumstances. It was the senseless waste in the destruction of innocence that affected him the most. These youngsters had not been in the world long enough to warrant suffering any harm, let alone their lives being snuffed out in such a vicious and violent fashion.

He stayed late at the office that night. Somehow he just couldn't face going home and pretending to return to some sort of normality, not when he knew it was up to him to prevent any more kids falling prey to this madman. He felt guilty enough after they had got nowhere after the first murder, but now he would really have to raise his game. This wasn't a one-off killer. The beast had started a pattern. There would be more bodies, more grieving parents, if he didn't come through.

A pattern.

He'd thought it, but hadn't seen it. With only two victims it would be difficult to see the big picture. But not impossible.

Well, he could try. Bloody hell, he had to try. And try damned hard.

Brewing up a particularly strong cup of coffee, he cleared his desk of all papers apart from those that dealt with the details concerning the two dead girls. Slowly he went through them, hoping that he could note down any similarity between them, anything, however small, that might link them. After half an hour he was struggling. The girls were roughly the same age. Their birthdays, May and July, were two months apart. However, they lived in different parts of the town and attended different schools. Gillian's father was a motor mechanic and her mother was a dental receptionist. Angela's father was an accountant and her mother worked as his secretary. The couples were not likely to socialise: they did not know each other and their social circles did not merge in any way. The girls both appeared to be average students at school. It seemed that Angela had some facility for music. She played the piano. That was about it.

Pattern? What pattern?

With a sigh he gazed down at the blank page of his notepad.

God, there had to be something.

Something.

He studied the notes again.

Some forty minutes later, Paul Snow left the building with the little seed of an idea planted in his brain. He had little hope that it would flower, but he would tend it carefully the next day.

The following morning was one of those bright spring days when the blue skies and sharp yellow sunshine led one to believe that summer had arrived early, until you felt the sharp edge to the wind that rustled the new leaves, chased scraps of paper down the pavement and cut through your clothing like a knife. Snow was in the office early. He was a poor sleeper at the best of times and when on a difficult investigation he found it impossible to sleep on beyond six. So he decided he would shower, breakfast and come into work. It was pointless just lying in bed, staring at the ceiling. And today he had that seed to attend to, to nurture with a bit of luck.

However, he had to wait for the arrival of DS Susan Morgan before he could take things further. She was on time as usual but he waited for her to grab herself the first tea of the day before calling her into his office. Initially there was an awkward moment between them. Snow could see from her apprehensive looks and uncertain body language that she was unsure what he was going to say to her.

To allay her fears that he might be about to touch on the personal conversation of a few days previously, he lifted up his case notes to indicate this was a business matter.

'I've been going through the background of the two girls,' he said. 'And I thought you might be able to help me.'

'Oh,' she seemed genuinely surprised.

'What do you know about the Marsdale Youth Choir?'

Susan looked surprised. This was certainly not the kind of question she was expecting.

'Marsdale Youth Choir?' she repeated, her brow gently wrinkling.

Snow nodded.

'Well, as far as I know it no longer exists. After the accident.'

'The accident. Oh, the coach crash.'

'Yes, it happened last winter. It was a kiddies' choir. Girls around the ages of nine and ten. They'd been entered into a competition over Manchester way. On the way back, their minibus crashed. A lot of the poor devils were killed.'

Snow nodded slowly. He was reminded that Melanie Bolton had mentioned the crash. Her daughter had been friends with one of the victims. For some reason Snow felt a small tingle of excitement.

'Why are you interested?' asked Susan.

Snow pursed his lips. 'Gillian Bolton and Angela Cleeves had both been members of the choir.'

'Really. Do you think that's significant?'

Snow shrugged. 'Possibly not, but as far as I can see that is the only slender thread that links the two girls.'

'Slender.'

'Can you get me the newspaper files on the accident and any other info on the choir? Presumably there are some adults still around who were involved.'

'Yes, sir. Will do,' she said. Her whole demeanour had altered now she was clearly and firmly in her role as police officer. Susan was very comfortable with this, and with a brisk movement, she left the office.

Within an hour, Susan had returned with a series of photocopies from the *Huddersfield Examiner* relating to the Marsdale Choir and the accident. Susan, in her usual efficient fashion, had organised them in date order.

Snow thanked her, grabbed himself a coffee and closed his office door, which was a sign to the other officers that he didn't want to be disturbed unless it was urgent. He then sat down to pore over the cuttings.

The first one read:

MARSDALE TOTS CONTENDERS FOR CLARION PRIZE

Huddersfield's prestigious youth singing group, the Marsdale Choir, have entered the Clarion Music Festival in Manchester in October. The group, made up of twelve young girls between the ages of nine and eleven, have already won some local trophies, including the Honley Singing Cup at the Honley Feast, and have high hopes of bringing away a prize from the Manchester competition. Choir mistress Mrs Gloria Niven (62) said the girls were very excited at entering the competition and were determined to prove their worth over the border in Lancashire. Marsdale Choir was only formed eighteen months ago but already it has achieved great acclaim and success. Part of the reason for the Choir's success is the mix of old and modern music in their repertoire. 'We tackle anything from Handel to the Beatles,' said Mrs Niven. There is now a long waiting list to join the choir, especially as they are booked to appear on BBC's local news programme *Look North* this Christmas with a fresh take on Irving Berlin's seasonal favourite, 'White Christmas'.

The second cutting included a picture showing the mangled remains of a minibus lying in a ditch in a moorland setting.

TRAGEDY ON MARSDALE MOOR

Eleven killed in terrible crash in fog

A tragic accident occurred last night in thick fog on the top of Marsdale Moor. A minibus, which was carrying the twelve members of the Marsdale Choir and some of their parents, skidded on the wet road surface in the fog and turned over and crashed down into a gulley. The driver, Francis Halford of Bradley Mills Lane, was killed along with the choir mistress, Mrs Gloria Niven of Greenlea Road, Slaithwaite. Seven young members of the choir also died in the crash, along with two parents: Mrs Aileen Dudley and Mrs Linda Green. The survivors were taken to Huddersfield General Hospital and were treated for comparatively minor injuries and allowed to go home.

A third cutting followed:

MEMORIAL SERVICE FOR THE
MARSDALE CRASH VICTIMS

The Reverend Archie Foster, vicar of Marsdale Parish Church, conducted the Memorial Service on Saturday for the victims of the horrendous crash which cruelly took away the lives of seven young girls, all members of the Marsdale Choir: Anne Green (10), Elaine Halstead (10), Lorna Blake (9), Brenda Truscott (11), Debbie Hirst (11), Zoe Blackmoore (10), Christine Dudley (11). Also amongst the fatalities were the driver, Francis Halford, Choir Mistress, Mrs Gloria Niven, Mrs Aileen Dudley and Mrs Linda Green.

The choir had just competed in the Clarion Music Festival in Manchester and were travelling home in a minibus when it ran into a patch of fog and crashed.

Thomas, the husband of Mrs Niven, was due to read a eulogy at the service but was too ill to attend. Rev Foster said that it would be many years before the dark shadow cast by this dreadful event would be erased. He praised the work of Mrs Niven and expressed his deepest sympathy for the parents who had lost their beloved daughters. Many left the church in tears.

Snow sat back and sighed. It was a terrible story. He remembered it but it had not really impinged on his consciousness. He had been involved in a complex investigation at the time and his mind and energies had been focused on that. He stared down at the cuttings again. Was there anything there? Two of the girls had been in the Marsdale Choir. They had survived the horrendous crash. They would have known each other. Was that a coincidence? Or …?

He pondered this conundrum for a while and then suddenly he sat back and gritted his teeth.

Time to get off my backside, he thought.

After his morning's activities, Snow grabbed a late lunch at the County: a beef sandwich and a half of Tetley's while he mulled over the events of the morning. He had visited both the mothers of the murdered children to ask them about the Marsdale Choir and if the two girls had been friends. It had not been a fruitful mission. According to Melanie Bolton, her daughter had mentioned Angela Cleeves but only in a disparaging way. 'I think Gill thought she was a bit stuck up. They certainly weren't mates.' On the other hand, Mrs Cleeves had told him that her daughter had never mentioned 'the Bolton girl' at all. Neither parent had been at the concert in Manchester.

If drawing a blank was an effective way of spending your morning, thought Snow, he'd done rather well.

Still the Marsdale Choir aspect of the case was, at the moment, the only glowing ember in a fairly dead bonfire, so he might as well blow a bit harder on it. Once he'd digested his rather dry and gristly sandwich, he planned to visit Thomas Niven, widower of the choirmistress.

The Nivens' house was a tidy bungalow on a quiet road on the outskirts of Marsdale, about four miles from Huddersfield. It always surprised and pleased Snow that once you had driven from the crowded centre of Huddersfield and were only a few miles from the town, on whichever road you took, you hit the countryside. Wooded hills rose around you, along with purple, rock-strewn moorland. You soon left the urban for the rural. To him they were complementary environments and in many ways it was what kept him in Huddersfield.

Marsdale was a charming community which, although close to Huddersfield, kept itself to itself. On his previous visits there, Snow has sensed that there was an air of insularity here borne out of self-preservation. They didn't want to be contaminated with town folk and their ways. There were no supermarkets or the usual imprints of the national high streets here. It was all small individual shops, run by locals – the butcher, the baker and, probably up a side street somewhere, a candlestick maker. Here was a simpler, old-fashioned way of living. The inhabitants seemed to relish that they were a little behind the times. Snow sympathised with their philosophy.

Snow made his way up the path, which cut its way through a neatly trimmed lawn, rang the door chimes and waited. A voice behind the frosted glass door called out: 'Just a minute, I'm coming.' Moments later, it opened to reveal a tall, thin man, stooped with age, with grey, lanky hair and a pair of steel-rimmed glasses on the end of his nose. He had a copy of the *Daily Telegraph* in his hand. Snow noted that it was folded at the crossword page. The man was dressed in cord trousers, a checked shirt and a fawn cardigan. He wore a pair of carpet slippers which looked too big for his feet.

'Yes?' he said, peering over the top of his glasses.

Snow held up his warrant card. 'I'm Detective Inspector Snow. I was wondering if I could have a word, sir?' He didn't, as some officers did, just hold up the card and snap 'Police' in an officious manner. Not only did he regard that as rude, mildly offensive, but he knew that it put people either on edge or on the defensive – neither attitude being conducive to extracting the right kind of information from the interviewee.

Mr Niven peered at the card. 'A word? What about?' He seemed confused.

'The accident and the choir.'

Niven groaned and ran his hand across the lower part of his face. 'Oh, Lord, not that again. Haven't I suffered enough? My wife was killed in that crash, you know.'

Snow nodded. 'I know, sir, but I think you might be able to help me with an investigation I'm involved in.'

'Investigation? What investigation?'

'Perhaps I could come in and talk to you, sir.'

Niven sighed. 'I suppose so.'

The sitting room to which Niven led him was somewhat untidy. It was, the policeman supposed, lacking the woman's touch. Snow was aware that when a man had been looked after all his life, he found it difficult to cope with the same precision on his own. And there didn't seem to be much point any more anyway. There was no one to see, was there? It had been the same with his father.

'Do move those magazines and sit down. You are an inspector, you say?'

'Yes, Detective Inspector with the West Yorkshire Police, based in Huddersfield.'

'I see. This must be serious then. Would you care for a cup of tea?'

'No, that's all right.'

Niven dropped into his armchair with another sigh. Snow could see that he was relieved not to have to fuss about in the kitchen, preparing mugs of tea and no doubt searching for some errant digestive biscuits to accompany them.

Snow assumed that Niven was in his late sixties, but he had the movement and demeanour of a much older man. He remembered the newspaper report which stated that he had been too ill to attend the memorial service for the crash victims. Maybe it wasn't just grief that kept him away but something more physical.

'Well, how do you think I can help you?'

'First of all, can you tell me about the Marsdale Choir?'

'Ah, that was my wife's pigeon. She should be here to tell you all about that.' He paused as though he had just realised what he'd said and he turned his head away and his body shook slightly. 'My God, I wish she was,' he muttered into his hand.

Snow waited a moment and then carried on matter-of-factly. He knew this was the best way to counteract that kind of emotion. 'I'm sure you helped her a lot with the youngsters.'

'Oh, yes, yes, I did.' He half-smiled. 'Well, I did as I was told. I was the unofficial gopher. Gloria had taught music at the local junior school until she retired early. She had quite a good little choir there and so she thought she'd try and set up an independent girls' choir and see if ... to use her words ... to see if they could "go places".' His grey face softened and he chuckled at the memory. 'She wanted the best, mind you. She was a stickler for perfection. That was the secret of her success. She held auditions and the candidates came from all areas of Huddersfield. Well, she had a bit of a reputation did my Gloria. Well deserved, too.'

Snow nodded. 'I am sure.'

'That was about two years ago and it wasn't very long before things started to happen. We won a few local competitions and then we started going further afield. The real success was the repertoire, you know. It was very broad and varied: a bit of "All in an April Evening" followed by some silly pop tune. There was no one else doing that. It was all Gloria's idea.'

'How were you involved?'

'As I said, as a dogsbody.' He gave a half-hearted salute and smiled but the sadness never quite left his eyes. 'I helped to arrange things in the background but I had nothing to do with the music side. I'm tone deaf. Can't hold a tune to save my life.' He gave another chesty chuckle.

'Did you get to know any of the girls?'

Thomas Niven raised his eyebrows in surprise. 'What do you mean?'

'Their characters and their individual talents. You must have got to know some of them quite well.'

'Not really. I was a backroom boy. Never went to rehearsals and that. Ran a few of them home sometimes but I was Mr Paperwork and Mr Phone Calls.'

'Did you know Gillian Bolton and Angela Cleeves?'

'Ah,' said Niven, his eyes widening, 'so that's where this is going. The two lasses who have been killed.'

Snow said nothing.

'I didn't know them. I knew of them. I saw them and I may have exchanged a few words with them, I suppose, like you do. But that's all.'

'Did your wife say anything about the girls?'

Niven thought for a moment. 'I believe she thought the Angela girl was particularly talented but a bit of a madam. My Glo ran those rehearsals like a military campaign. From the moment the girls arrived until they left, it was work, work, work. That's why they were so bloody good. There was no time to chit chat or fool about. I doubt if any firm friendships sprang up through the choir.'

'Why didn't you go to the concert in Manchester on the night of the crash?'

'I wasn't well enough. I was recovering from chemo. I had cancer. I've still bloody well got it. Some bugger up there deemed it appropriate that I should carry on living in discomfort while my Gloria, who had nothing wrong with her and so much to give, should die.' Angry tears now rolled down the old man's ashen features and he clenched his hands together in a desperate attempt to control his emotions.

These scenes embarrassed Snow. He never knew what to say. He felt sorry for Niven, empathised with him even, but he knew that nothing he could say would ease his pain. That practical rationale prevented him from reaching out in any sentimental, empty-gestured fashion to Niven. He should have brought Susan with him. She knew how to handle these situations. She could with great skill and remarkable facility both comfort and elicit information from the distressed interviewee.

'It were terrible, y'know. That crash,' Niven said suddenly, sniffing back the tears, his back straightening as he stared ahead of him, as though he was witnessing the accident in his mind. Although he hadn't been there, Snow assumed that he must have formed images of what happened from all the reports he had heard and read. 'Seven girls died that night,' he continued. 'Seven young lives snuffed out. Terrible. Most of the parents had gone by car to Manchester because there wasn't room on the coach. Aileen Dudley and Linda Green drew the short straw. They copped it, along with the driver. Mind you, I reckon he was to blame, y'know. He was obviously going too fast. It's a bad road at night over the tops, especially in the dark, and susceptible to mist patches. He'd have known that. And they found alcohol in his bloodstream, y'know, so he'd obviously had a drink or two. How could he? In charge of a bus full of youngsters? The bastard.'

Snow nodded. He knew that the general consensus was that the driver was probably the cause of the crash, despite the coroner's verdict of death by misadventure.

'And, do you know, the tragedy didn't end there – there out on those cold damp moors.'

Snow shook his head gently. 'What do you mean?'

'Debbie Hirst, one of the lasses who copped it that night. Her mother topped herself. She couldn't stand the pain of the loss. It was too much for her so she clambered up on a bridge over the M62 and jumped off. Terrible, isn't it? What the cruel death of someone dear to you can do. It messes up your mind. But I tell you this, Inspector, I wish I'd been on the coach that night. It would have been better if we'd gone together, Glo and I. I miss her so much it bloody well hurts – hurts more than the cancer.

There's nothing here for me now. We had no children of our own so I'm left here with nothing. Nothing but the telly and the crossword, biding my time, waiting for death, waiting for the damned cancer to finally claim me.'

When Snow got back to the office, he found Bob Fellows hovering around his office door with a big grin plastered across his face.

'Bit of a breakthrough, boss.'

'Go on.'

'That lass, Miranda Stone … She's seen the van again. And she got its number.'

A small electric thrill ran through Snow's body. This was potentially very good news indeed.

'Tell me more.'

'Well, the girl was in town and she saw the van. She recognised it.'

'Because of its colour and the Blackpool sticker she mentioned?'

'The colour, yes, but inevitably the sticker had been removed, but she looked closely and saw the triangular outline where it had been.'

'Clever girl.'

'Very clever because she also had the presence of mind to write down the number plate this time.'

'Excellent. Did she see the driver?'

Bob shook his head. ' Apparently the van was empty. She was on her own and she was too scared to hang around.'

'Very sensible of her but a pity she didn't get a glimpse of him. Where was the van parked?'

'At the top of town near the ABC cinema.'

'Have you traced it yet?'

'We're on it now.'

'Well,' said Snow, 'that's potentially the best bit of news we've had for a while.'

The word 'potentially'. Snow knew not to be so sanguine in situations like this. Some clues were like bubbles: you could chase them a while but if you tried to manhandle them, they vanished into thin air. As it turned out in this case, his cynical vibes proved accurate. This potential break in the case was too good to be true. An hour later, Bob came to his office, his face gloomy and shoulders hunched.

'The van was reported stolen from a garage forecourt a month ago,' he said without preamble.

Snow nodded. 'It was to be expected, I suppose, but one always lives in hope.'

'Hope is the bread and butter of the police force.'

Snow raised his eyebrows at this observation. 'Is that the family motto?'

Bob smiled. 'Sort of, actually. My dad used to say that all the time. He was only a humble PC but he knew the form.'

'I reckon he did. Well, at least we've learned that our fellow hasn't left the scene. He's still around Huddersfield, so get a message out to the troops to be extra vigilant. If a little girl can spot the van on a busy street in town, God help us, one of our sharp-eyed coppers should be able to match her.'

Bob gave a salute. 'It shall be done.'

'We'd better hold the number back from the press for the time being. Once it becomes public, the devil will ditch the van immediately.'

'Good thinking, sir.'

When he was alone again, Snow glanced at his watch. It was well after five now. He was weary and ready to call it a day. The thought of trudging home and making himself some makeshift meal filled him with gloom. His cooking skills were limited at the best of times and the way he felt now, he reckoned he'd make a mess of a cheese sandwich, let alone anything more ambitious. He decided on the spur of the moment to treat himself to an Indian. It had been a while since he'd been to the Shabab and he reckoned that a spicy madras curry would go down a treat. It might well help to spice up his thinking on the case.

The Shabab was only a five-minute walk from police HQ and Snow enjoyed the stroll, breathing in the cool early evening air. He walked through the door at the restaurant just after six. The atmosphere was heady with rich and pungent spices, and before he had been shown to his table, their potency had made him feel very hungry. He ordered a lager while he perused the menu. At this stage of the evening, the restaurant was quiet, with many empty tables. There were several solitary diners, individuals like himself, Snow assumed, with no one at home to share a meal with. It was times like this that he realised how isolated he was. There was no one close to him. No one whom he could confide in, to hold him tightly, to love him. The combination of his job and his sexuality made it essential that he kept that invisible barrier, that shield as he thought of it, around himself in order to function and survive. But it was times like this, sitting alone in a restaurant, that his heart ached for companionship – for some sort of ordinary life.

He ordered a chicken madras curry and another lager from the young, attentive Asian waiter and then tried to turn his thoughts away from himself and return to his current investigation. It wasn't easy and, as he struggled with his mindset, a shadow fell across his table and a voice addressed him.

'Hello again,' it said, softly but in a cheerful tone.

Snow looked up and saw Colin Bird standing by his table. 'I thought it was you,' he said.

Snow nodded. 'Yes, it's me. Last time I looked anyway.'

'On your own?'

Snow looked around him. 'Seem to be,' he said, hating himself for all this forced irony.

Bird gave him an indulgent grin and Snow knew what was coming next. He also knew what he would have to say.

'Well, do you mind if I join you?' It was now his turn to gaze around in an exaggerated fashion. 'It seems that I'm on my own, too.'

Snow grinned. 'Help yourself,' he found himself saying, indicating the chair beside him.

Bird sat down. 'Thanks. I've been promising myself a curry all day. It was the only way I could tolerate the pile of paperwork that's been dumped on my desk. It's little treats that keep you going in this job. I bet you're the same.'

'Sort of,' replied Snow. 'I thought I'd give the microwave a rest tonight.'

Bird nodded. 'I know what you mean.'

God, thought Snow, how long can this excruciating bloody small talk go on? Instead of a relaxing meal, this was going to be sheer torture.

'We must stop bumping into each other like this,' said Bird suddenly. There was no lightness of touch or humour in his voice. 'Here and Sherwood's. Do you go there often?'

Trick question, thought Snow. He wasn't sure what this guy was after — on which side of the divide he stood.

In response, he gave a slight shake of the head, hoping that would draw a line under the subject.

'I like it a lot,' said Bird, leaning forward, his unblinking stare focused on Snow. 'A lot,' he repeated.

At this point the waiter arrived to take Bird's order. Snow was irked that he was now lumbered with a dining companion he didn't want and one that was probing a little too delicately for his liking. What was his game?

He took a gulp of cool lager to help steady his nerves. The food ordered, the two men sat back and for a moment there was an uncomfortable silence. Snow had no real idea which way to take the conversation. He certainly wanted to move it away from anything personal. Either this man was probing about his sexual predilections with a view to exposing him or – and this thought surprised him when it came unbidden to his mind – he was a gay man seeking a friend of the same persuasion.

'You're on these nasty murders of the two young lasses at the moment, aren't you?' Bird said at last.

How the devil did he know that? thought Snow. He must have been checking up on him.

'Yes,' he nodded. 'It's a difficult one.'

'Motive?'

'Not established yet. I'm convinced the crimes aren't random but the link between the victims is fragile, tentative.' Snow was relieved that the conversation had shifted to police work – it was certainly more comfortable than the subject of Sherwood's and its implications – but he didn't care to discuss his investigations in detail, especially with someone who was not on his team. 'What about yourself?' he asked, hoping to move the focus.

Bird smiled. 'Same old. Same old. Very routine stuff in our neck of the woods. Nothing glamorous like a grisly homicide.'

Snow gave a sour grin. 'Nothing glamorous about it, I assure you. There are some days when I'd gladly be racing down the M62 doling out a few speeding tickets.' Both men laughed and the atmosphere eased.

Later on, thinking back over the evening, Snow could not quite pinpoint exactly when things got easier, more relaxed and friendly, nor what he and Bird actually talked about. He knew that Sherwood's never came up again and that he managed to steer clear of his murder case, but the rest had evaporated from his memory. However, it was true that, with a warm curry inside him and a couple more lagers, he felt surprisingly relaxed and comfortable in the company of Colin Bird. He was a few years younger than Snow, with short cropped blond hair topping a pugnacious but not unpleasant face, which bore what his father would have called 'a Roman nose – roamin' all over his face'. Bird was somewhat on the heavy side and possessed a certain charm which Snow observed he could switch on and off as it pleased him.

It was dark as the two men emerged from the restaurant. Snow was aware that he was slightly over the alcoholic limit to drive home and so was his dining companion.

'Taxis for both of us, I think.'

'Are you saying we call it a night …?'

'I think we must. Well, I must. I need to be fresh and on my toes in the morning.'

'Ah, work: the curse of the drinking classes.'

The two men laughed.

'We must do this again,' said Colin, squeezing Snow's arm.

'Sure.' And Snow surprised himself by meaning it.

ELEVEN

He knew he should wait. Wait longer. His common-sense instincts told him that. Screamed at him that this was the case, but as usual he knew he was going to let his emotions overrule the caution. He was eager to complete his task. He wanted it to be over. He needed to finish what he had started before he was caught. That would spoil everything. And 'waiting for the dust to settle', the phrase he used to himself, would only give the police greater time to collect clues, sum up evidence and be on to him. No, he convinced himself, he needed to get on with things. Strike while his emotions were hot. He needed to commit the next murder.

Asia Chowdry left her group of friends in the playground and with some reluctance set her feet for home. It was annoying to her that she had no time to have fun with her schoolmates. She had duties at home to perform. As her mother was fond of telling her, she was part of the family and therefore she had to serve the family. Serve meant cleaning, looking after her younger brother and making meals for granny, who was now too ill to come downstairs.

'Once your schooling is done, you must come straight home and help in the home. It is your duty, young lady.'

'Yes, mother,' she would reply, avoiding the fearsome gaze and staring at the floor. It was inappropriate to show her resentment at being treated like a servant, but she felt it all the same.

Refusal was out of the question. But resentment was not.

Asia cast an envious glance back at the playground where her friends, noisy and animated, were having a great time. Ginny Bradshaw waved at her and smiled.

Asia returned the gesture in a half-hearted fashion and then turned her back and began to move away. If she was late, she would get a scolding. As she trudged along the street, she had no notion that a van was keeping pace with her. She also had no notion that she would not get home that night, or any other night.

Snow received the call around eight that evening. He was just about to sit down and watch some mindless television programme for an hour or so before heading for bed. As a man with no family and few friends, he knew that an evening call could mean only one thing. It was professional. And that meant trouble.

It was Susan on the line. In her businesslike manner, she gave him the gist. A girl had been reported missing. She was of a similar age to the two who had been murdered. Asia Chowdry was her name. A good girl. The mother was distraught.

There was nothing definite, of course, but they both knew they could not ignore the possibility that there was a link with the murder case.

'Keep me up to speed if there are any developments,' he said.

'Of course, sir.'

They both knew what 'developments' really meant. Snow's heart was heavy as he replaced the receiver. So soon. Not another dead girl. Please, God, no.

And then something sparked in Snow's brain. It was the girl's name. It was beautiful and unusual: Asia. So unusual that he remembered it.

Or thought that he had.

With lightning speed he rushed to the hallway and retrieved his case notes from his briefcase which he had abandoned there. Returning to the sitting room, he sat on the edge of the sofa and riffled through the sheets of paper until he found the page that he wanted.

He stared at it open mouthed. My God, that slender thread he had talked about had suddenly become much stronger. He gazed down at the names on the list: Gillian Bolton, Angela Cleeves and Asia Chowdry had all been on the coach that fatal night when the crash had occurred. They had been on the coach and they had survived.

Was this crazy bastard picking off those young kids who had lived? If this were the case, this was madness heaped upon madness. Snow closed his eyes and shook his head, hoping that he was wrong.

Slowly he moved into the kitchen and made himself a strong coffee and read through the whole set of case files again.

About the time Snow was trawling through his notes, PC Alan Hargreaves was walking his beat around the old Beast Market area of Huddersfield, down at the bottom of town. He was conscientious but bored. He hadn't joined the force to pound the pavement, although he knew that this was inevitably part of the process of becoming a proper policeman. You had to serve your time on the streets before you could contemplate going plain clothes. He'd been doing this for six months now and for his pains he had arrested two drunks, a soliciting tart and a flasher. Hardly the Sweeney, was it, he moaned to his mates. And they had laughed. He knew he'd have to pay his time, as his sergeant was always telling him, but it still did not stop him being impatient.

As he passed down by the Huddersfield Hotel, he saw the van. It appeared to have stalled by the traffic lights. The engine was 'coughing its guts up', as Hargreaves later reported, black smoke billowing out of its exhaust, but it was refusing to function. Hargreaves stood at some distance, observing the vehicle for a while. In some ways it fitted the description of the one they had all been told to keep a sharp eye out for. It was a dull, light-brown Ford transit with a rusty bumper. His hand reached for his breast pocket to bring out his notebook and check the registration number against the one he had been given. Unbuttoning the pocket, he felt inside. The notebook was not there.

'Shit!' he cursed violently. He remembered immediately that he had taken it out at the station to note something down and had placed it casually on the top of his locker. That's where it still was. He could see it in his mind's eye – taunting him.

'Shit,' he said again.

Still, he did remember that there were 4 and 3 involved and the vehicle before him had such numbers on its dirty registration plate. And he remembered that there was something about the outline of a triangular sticker on the back.

With some excitement, PC Hargreaves drew closer to the van and saw that there was indeed a triangular outline on the rear window where a pennant had once been. And the window was blacked out. The back of Hargreaves' neck began to tingle and his heart began to thud against his chest as he realised the importance of this moment. With some deliberation he moved into the road and walked around to the driver's side and tapped gently on the window.

The man inside, his features indistinct in the dully illuminated cab, was busily turning the ignition key and thumping the accelerator in a desperate attempt to get the thing moving but the engine just whined and juddered to no effect. The policeman's arrival and tap on the window pane made the man jump and he emitted a sharp cry of shock.

Hargreaves made a miming motion to indicate that the driver should wind his window down. Instead of doing so, the driver pulled back into the shadows of the cab.

'Open up, please sir,' ordered Hargreaves.

But the man seemed to have disappeared from sight. The policeman tried the handle but the door was locked and then, to his surprise, he saw the door at the far side of the vehicle swing open.

My God, thought Hargreaves, the bugger's getting out the passenger's side. *He's making a run for it.*

The policeman raced around the front of the van in time to see the driver sprinting down the street. Hargreaves gave chase. His quarry had a good thirty yards' lead on him, but the fleet-footed copper soon began to gain ground. And then suddenly, the man slowed down and ran up the steps of an adjacent building and disappeared inside. It was the entrance to the Huddersfield Hotel.

'Gotcher!' cried Hargreaves with a grin.

However, on entering the hotel the policeman encountered three doors, each neatly labelled in gothic script: one was down into the 'Restaurant', one to the 'Lavatories' and one led up a small flight of stairs to the 'Reception'.

He hesitated for a moment, unsure which one to take before making his way into the reception area. The girl behind the desk was drinking coffee and idly flipping through the pages of a magazine. She glanced up at his approach and seemed surprised to see a bulky officer of the law, somewhat red of face and perspiring, bearing down on her.

'Has a man passed through here just now?' he barked at her without any preamble.

The girl shivered at his brusqueness. 'Just now?' she repeated with some bewilderment.

'Yes. A scruffy chap with a beard … I think.'

'In the last few minutes.'

Hargreaves rolled his eyes. He wanted to slap the stupid girl. 'Yes,' he snapped.

She shook her head. She was about to add, 'I ain't seen nobody for at least half an hour,' but the policeman was already heading for the door.

His heart was heavy as he entered the restaurant, which was empty. Business was bad. A waiter approached him. 'A table for one, sir.'

Hargreaves shook his head. 'I'm looking for a man, a scruffy man. Has anyone been in here in the last few minutes?'

The waiter seemed to take a while to assimilate this information, but when he had, he nodded his head in the affirmative. 'Oh, yes, clumsy bloke. He ran in, knocked over a chair and went into the kitchen.' The waiter pointed to a door at the far end of the restaurant. Hargreaves was through the door in a trice. There were two cooks and a waitress huddled in a group, chatting. They turned with mild interest at Hargreaves' entrance.

He cut to the chase. 'Where did the man go?' he asked sharply.

Without a word, all three pointed to the side door, which was slightly ajar. Hargreaves discovered that it led to a small yard and from there freedom for his quarry.

'Bollocks,' he hissed in frustration.

The man had escaped.

In fact, in truth, he had allowed the man to escape. That was the truth of the matter. What chance had he now to curtail his days of feet-pounding on the beat? He swore violently under his breath, before returning to the kitchen where he discovered the trio had resumed their conversation. Business was obviously slow and their curiosity level was zero. They did not give him a cursory glance as he pushed past them and through into the restaurant.

With a heavy heart, the policeman returned to the abandoned vehicle while radioing HQ to give them a brief resumé about what had happened. Without bending the truth, he lessened the elements of what he considered was his incompetence. However, he realised with a leaden heart that anyone scrutinising the basic outline of events could see that he had been found wanting.

Slipping the keys from the ignition, PC Hargreaves moved to the back of the van and unlocked the doors. The interior was empty apart from a pile of sacking at the far end. Hargreaves clambered inside and examined this. His stomach churned and he felt his bile rise when he pulled back the roll of sacking. It revealed the body of a young Asian girl beneath. She was bound and gagged and lay in a foetal position. He felt for a pulse. There wasn't one.

The full implication of the situation made PC Hargreaves cry out in anguish. The girl was dead and he had just allowed her murderer to escape.

TWELVE

Snow allowed the steaming hot coffee to burn the back of his throat. The discomfort was somehow satisfying. It was early the following morning and he was reading PC Hargreaves' report. Already the staff at the Huddersfield Hotel had been interviewed, but it seemed to Snow that they were not only blind and deaf but also in some way brain-damaged. None of them could give any details as to the appearance of the man who ran through the premises in a frantic manner. Each one seemed to have encountered a different fellow who was able to change his shape from tall to short and well-built to thin, and the jury was out as to his age and colouring. Even Hargreaves himself wasn't much better, using terms like 'shadowy figure', 'believed to have a beard', 'shabby clothing' and 'average height and build'.

And the little girl was dead.

She had been killed in the same manner as the other two. She had been chloroformed and then strangled. No doubt the killer was on his way to some lonely beauty spot to dump her body when the van had given up the ghost. Hargreaves had been so close to bringing this case to an end. So close, but … what did the Americans say? No cigar.

Snow sighed. Fate had a way of rubbing one's face in the mud now and then. Actually not that infrequently: most of the time really.

The van was being picked over by forensics and you never knew, there might be some clue as to the identity of this bastard who was killing little girls. Sadly, Snow felt he did know – he knew they wouldn't find anything of real significance because this fellow was clever and meticulous. And, more importantly, it was clear to Snow that he was fully focused on his murderous occupation. Nothing else mattered to him. His mind was tuned into this channel only and protecting his identity was one of the key elements of his operations.

Another mouthful of hot coffee. Snow wasn't usually this pessimistic but there was something about this case that had robbed him of any sanguinity. He was also suffering from the burden of guilt that he felt for not catching this bastard. Logically, he could not have saved the first girl, but now there were two other corpses and realistically they were no nearer catching the killer than they had been on day one. And, for Christ's sake, he was the senior investigating officer. The buck really stopped with him.

At least now he had a thread with which to link the murders. All three girls had been members of the Marsdale Choir and had survived the crash on the moors. For some reason the killer was picking off these girls. There were two survivors left: Elizabeth Saunders and Teresa Duff. They were now in danger. Great danger, because the killer would be very spooked by his close call and realise how vulnerable his position had become. Also he would know that by now the police would have worked out the connection between each of the murdered girls and would be able to put measures in place to protect the two potential victims. As a result he'd want to get the job – his mission – over with as quickly as possible. And Snow felt it was a mission. Something was driving this man to kill these girls as though he wanted to obliterate all of the choir. He was carrying out the task with almost religious zeal. And Snow was sure that the remaining two surviving girls were to be his next targets.

He had organised for surveillance on the girls' homes and female police officers to accompany them to school. Pictures of the van had appeared on the television news with the hope that some viewers would recognise the vehicle and contact the police. Someone must know where the bastard was hanging out.

Despite everything, it was still a waiting game.

What really haunted and frustrated Snow was the mystery of this man's motives. Why did he want to kill perfectly innocent girls? It was like he was desperate to eradicate all traces of the choir, as though it had never existed. For what reason? The choir was the link but why? He drained his coffee mug and grimaced. In this case it wasn't just a matter of thinking out of the box, it was eliminating the box altogether.

Amos Rawcliffe struggled vainly with the recalcitrant door of the telephone box. 'Bloody hell,' he wheezed in panting frustration. 'Don't they bloody well want you to make a frigging phone call?'

A fine rain was falling and the weather was unseason-ably cold. Amos was all about ready to give up trying to get into the phone box when the door finally gave a little on its stiff over-painted hinges and he was able to squeeze himself through the gap. He virtually fell inside, slumping against the side of the tiny receptacle.

'Bloody hell,' he said again when he had recovered enough breath to speak. Why on earth had he believed that this was a good idea, he thought. God only knows. Instinctively he gazed heavenwards. 'Don't you?' he said, addressing the invisible almighty. 'And when I'm done are you going to let me get out of this frigging goldfish bowl?'

After a few moments, Amos pulled himself upright and mopped his brow, which despite the cold was dappled with sweat. He searched in his pockets for the scrap of paper on which he'd written down the number. After a while, he retrieved it but then realised that he couldn't read his own spidery seventy-five-year-old handwriting without the aid of his spectacles.

'Frigging hell,' he moaned again as he rummaged inside his variety of jacket pockets in search of his reading glasses. As he placed them on his nose, they steamed up, misting his vision. This prompted another oath.

The atmosphere inside the phone box was rank. Amos thought of it as a mixture of cat wee, dog shit and sweat, and now the small panes of glass were all steamed up so that he really felt he was in some noxious cell, forever trapped in this foul-smelling coffin.

'Let's get the bloody thing over with,' he said as he lifted the receiver and dialled.

'Hello, hello,' he said imperiously when the call was answered at the other end. 'It's about that thing in the paper. That thing about the van you've been after. I know where it came from. I know who owns it. You want to know, don't you? This is the police I'm talking to, isn't it?'

Paul Snow and Bob Fellows sat tentatively on the edge of the settee in Amos Rawcliffe's sitting room. To Snow's mind, the place had probably not seen a tidy, a vacuum cleaner or a duster since the war. How could anyone live in such chaos? Looking over at old Amos, sitting back in the shabbiest armchair he had ever encountered, cradling a cup and saucer in his lap, it was obvious that this ragged old fellow could. In fact not only did he seem quite content in his surroundings, but he appeared completely oblivious of the squalor that surrounded him. He slurped his tea contentedly. Snow and Fellows had not been offered refreshment, which to Snow was a relief. Who knew exactly what the old man was drinking and how long it had been lurking in the kitchen?

'He called himself John Hall,' Rawcliffe continued, 'and paid me ten pounds a week for the use of the land to park his caravan on it. He was no bother but I thought there was something shifty about him. I was a school caretaker in my time and I came across a lot of wrong 'uns in them days. I prided myself in being able to spot 'em. Little bastards with mischief on their mind. I felt a bit the same about him, this John Hall. He never quite looked me in the face. Avoided my glances. Still I never questioned where he'd come from or why he'd landed up here. None of my business as long as he paid up regularly, which he did.'

'Can you describe him? What did he look like?' asked Snow.

Rawcliffe screwed up his face in an act of recollection. 'He was a sturdy bloke, not fat, just sturdy. In his fifties, I should guess. He had a beard and longish hair and sometimes he wore glasses – those big horn-rimmed things.' He paused and screwed his face up further. 'He was from round here, I reckon. You could tell that by his accent. There was really nowt special about him. You'd pass him in the street and not notice him.'

'How long ago did he come here?'

'Oh, about two, three months maybe. To be honest, I didn't see much of him, but I made it a point to go round every Thursday night for the rent and I'd inspect the place to see everything was OK, like. You can see the caravan from that window over there. It's parked on that patch of ground just beyond the wall. It was my allotment once upon a time when my Cheryl was alive and me legs worked properly. It's been idle for eight years or more. When this Hall chap came and asked if he could park there, I thought why not? Forty quid a month will do me very nicely.'

Instinctively the two men rose and moved to the window and gazed out. As described, just beyond the old stone garden wall was the rusting caravan.

'I've not seen him for a couple of days now. His van's not been parked up since Tuesday. I reckon he's done a bunk.'

'I reckon you're right,' muttered Bob Fellows, more to himself than to Rawcliffe.

Snow nodded at his colleague. It was clear that the old fellow was not a crank and it was possible that this was a serious lead. 'We'd better get the SOCOs up here pronto,' he said. 'They should be able to come up with something to help us trace him.'

'What's he done? Why are you after him?' asked Rawcliffe, a touch of fear in his voice.

'Nothing that need bother you at the moment,' said Snow, not unkindly. 'But I must ask you not to venture into the caravan till our boys have had a chance to inspect it. OK?'

Rawcliffe nodded, his eyes wide with apprehension. 'I knew he were a wrong 'un.'

Once outside the little cottage, Snow wandered to the garden wall and gazed at the old caravan. What secrets did it hold? Would something inside lead them to the killer? It was very tempting to clamber over the wall and have a look inside but he knew such an action was against the rules. He would be contaminating what was possibly a crime scene. He would just have to be patient.

Mrs Eva Hodge could not afford to be fussy regarding her 'paying guests', as she referred to her lodgers, for she knew her 'facilities' were of the basic quality. A small room with bed, cheap wardrobe, chest of drawers and the use of a communal bathroom and toilet. However, as she gazed at the man on her doorstep she was indeed tempted to be fussy. He was scruffy and somewhat dishevelled with the minimum of luggage – this was usual with her transient customers, fellows living on the edge of solvency – but there was something rather chilling in his demeanour and in particular in those pale watery eyes, which, as they gazed at her, seemed to be seeing something else, something beyond her. His voice was low and rasping, almost a whisper, as though he was unused to speaking. She wondered if he was an ex-con.

'How long are you wanting to stay?' Eva Hodge asked.

The man shrugged. 'A couple of weeks, I guess,' he said and held up a clutch of pound notes. 'That should cover it?' he said.

At the sight of the money, Mrs Hodges' growing resolve to refuse him melted away. 'I don't allow visitors or cooking in the rooms,' she said, her hand snaking out to lift the money from the man's hand.

The man nodded and edged forward into the hallway.

THIRTEEN

In many ways, Paul Snow was a creature of habit. There were certain routines built into his life which he adhered to whenever possible. Sometimes the dictates of his job meant he had to alter or adjust these routines and this caused him some dismay. He had long adopted the habit of carrying out his weekly shop at Lodges supermarket in Birkby early on Thursday morning before he went into work. He hated shopping for groceries and household items and he made sure that he bought all he needed for the next seven days with one visit. There was no dilly-dallying down the aisles for him, checking the relative prices of goods. He got in there, bought his stuff and left. And that's what he intended to do on this occasion until a hand fell on his shoulder by the meat counter.

'I can recommend the apple and pork sausages. They're particularly tasty,' said a voice in his ear, which broke in on his focused concentration.

Snow turned awkwardly to find himself facing Colin Bird. Playfully Bird rammed Snow's trolley with his. 'Snap,' he grinned.

'Hello,' said Snow, a little nonplussed to see Bird in this unusual environment.

'Do you come here often?' quipped Bird.

Snow smiled. 'Not if I can help it,' he said.

'Bugger, isn't it, shopping for one?'

Snow nodded. 'Shopping, full stop.'

'You nearly done?'

Snow gazed at his trolley. 'Sort of. Just one or two more things …'

'What say I treat you to a coffee in the little cafe. See you there in ten minutes, eh? Good man.'

He went before Snow had chance to respond.

Fifteen minutes later he was sitting at a cramped table in the cafe area with Colin Bird, who had not only bought the coffees but also what Snow regarded as a revolting synthetic cream doughnut. He had no intention of eating it all. He took a small mouthful to be polite and then slipped the plate to the side, hidden by the plastic menu.

'So are you a regular at Lodges?' asked Snow, for want of anything better to say.

'Not as much as you,' Bird observed slyly. 'Anyway, I'm glad I've seen you. I've … I've got a bit of a proposition to put to you.' He wrinkled his nose and shook his head. 'Nah, not proposition. That sounds a bit dodgy, doesn't it? It's all this police speak we're used to spouting. I meant an offer. An invitation …'

Snow took a sip of coffee and said nothing.

'I thought it would be fun if you and I took a trip to Sherwood's on Saturday night. What d'you say?'

Snow didn't say anything for a while. He couldn't believe Bird could be so crass. 'I think not,' he said evenly.

'Why not?'

'No.'

'You're not going to tell me it's not your scene, are you?' Bird's voice had darkened now and the humour had left his eyes. 'Because I know it is.'

'We shall have to beg to differ then,' said Snow, rising from his seat. 'Thanks for the coffee.'

Bird grabbed his arm tightly. 'You can't go like that. For fuck's sake, Paul, you've got to live a little. You can't live in a straitjacket all your life.'

Snow yanked his arm free from Bird's grip. 'As I said: thanks for the coffee,' he said coolly, and walked away.

As he walked to the car park with his trolley, Paul Snow's heart was beating furiously.

From the window of his cottage, Amos Rawcliffe watched with fascination as the Scenes of Crime Officers buzzed like flies around a jam pot, investigating the abandoned caravan on his land. They were dusting the door with powder, taking numerous photographs, popping in and out the van at regular intervals, carrying with them polythene bags containing items which they took away to a waiting police vehicle. The inspector and his assistant stood quietly nearby, watching this frenzied activity.

What on earth had that John Hall done? John Hall? Well, that obviously wasn't his real name. He must have carried out some really terrible crime to warrant all this fevered activity. Amos suddenly shuddered as a thought struck him. Friggin' hell, he could have been a killer. I could have been murdered in my bed. I reckon I've had a friggin' lucky escape.

Outside, Snow stood quietly by the caravan while the SOCOs got on with the job. Sean Quigley, the officer in charge, appeared at the door and beckoned to him.

'There's nothing of obvious significance as I can see, sir,' he said. 'The guy has covered his tracks very carefully. It's as though he was expecting the caravan to be found.'

Snow nodded to indicate that this assessment was in line with his own thinking.

'However …' Quigley allowed himself a brief smile. 'I have found something.' With a cheesy dramatic gesture, reminiscent of an end-of-the-pier magician, he produced a transparent polythene envelope from behind his back. It contained two black and white photographs. Snow took the envelope and scrutinised the photographs. One, the smaller of the two, was an informal snap of a young girl aged around eight years old. She was smiling at the camera in a shy way. It was very fuzzy and her features were in shadow but there was something about the girl that struck a chord with Snow – but he didn't know what. He had seen a copy of the other photograph before. It was a more formal shot of the Marsdale Choir. What was rather chilling was that all the faces of the young girls, apart from two, had a black cross marked across their faces.

Snow gave an involuntary shudder.

'Where did you find these?'

'Under the knifebox in the kitchen drawer, covered up by an old tea towel.'

'Get these tested for fingerprints and then let me have them pronto. I want to find the identity of this girl.'

'Will do,' said Quigley, puffing out his chest a little. He knew he had hit some kind of jackpot.

He sat near the school gates in his new van – new to him, that was. This rattle trap was at least fifteen years old and probably wouldn't make it to sixteen. But it had been all he could afford. Money was running out now and he still had his mission to complete. Two more deaths to arrange. And it wasn't going to be easy. Not now. The police were obviously on to his game. He could see Elizabeth Saunders accompanied by a police officer collecting her from school. Obviously she was there to protect the girl. The cops had worked out that she was a probable target, which meant they were putting the pieces of the puzzle together. Very soon they would get to the key missing piece: him.

The policewoman took hold of the girl's hand, chatting in a jolly fashion as she led her to the police car at the end of the road. They drove off, disappearing into a stream of traffic.

What the hell was he to do now? How could he get to the girl? No doubt the other one would be similarly chaperoned. He knew that he hadn't the luxury of time to wait. He needed to act fast. Doors were shutting in his face very quickly. Something drastic had to be done. What, he wasn't quite sure yet, but he now accepted that others might have to be harmed in the process. He had realised very early on that this might be the case and he must not flinch now. He must not be stopped in his mission. After all, he had the right of justice on his side.

Paul Snow had just started washing up after his evening meal when the doorbell rang. He frowned and moved to the front door apprehensively. He never had unexpected visitors in the evening unless they were connected with work, and even then this was rare. A phone call was the usual summons to drag him back from his spartan domesticity to the grubby world of crime.

He discovered Colin Bird on the doorstep, wearing a broad grin and clutching a bottle of red wine in his hand.

'Surprise!' he chortled, thrusting the bottle towards Snow. 'Avon calling.'

For a moment Snow was lost for words, although he was able to deduce that Bird was not quite sober: the misty eyes, the slightly slurred speech and the dishevelled tie told him as much.

Bird filled in the gap left by Snow's lack of response. 'Aren't you going to invite me in?'

It was the last thing Snow wanted to do, but he felt it was the safest under the circumstances. A tipsy colleague on his doorstep with a bottle of wine would not be an ideal scenario.

'I thought you and I could have a little drink,' Bird muttered as he followed Snow into the sitting room.

'Have you driven here?'

Bird giggled. 'Still on duty, eh? Nah, got a taxi. Not stupid, old boy.'

'What brings you here?' As soon as the words left his mouth, Snow regretted uttering them.

'A social call. Come to see my old buddy, well new buddy really. I thought a few drinks might cement the relationship. Might act as a little persuader … eh?'

'Maybe you've already had your few drinks.'

'Don't you believe it.' Suddenly Bird's voice seemed more assured, less indistinct. The squiffy entrance had been faked. To cover embarrassment? To ensure entry? Snow could not be sure, but there was some nasty devious game being played here.

'Now we'll need two glasses and a corkscrew. Come on, Paul, hurry up. This is a damn fine wine and it's eager to be sampled.'

Without a word, Snow went into the kitchen to retrieve the glasses and corkscrew. He didn't quite know what was going on here, although rather worriedly he had his suspicions. And he didn't like it. He didn't like it one bit. He knew that he would have to be civil, or as civil as circumstances would allow, but he had to get rid of his visitor as soon as possible. No doubt a visit to Sherwood's would raise its head again and he would have to ride that particular awkward roller.

When Snow returned to the sitting room, he found Bird had taken off his jacket and tie and was perusing the bookcase. 'A love of Dickens, I see.' The voice was now normal with no trace of inebriation.

'Amongst others.'

'No Thomas Hardy, I see.'

'Too fatalistic for my taste. You've got to give people a chance. We're not puppets. Fate may play about with us, deal us blows, but we also have free will, otherwise we'd all be slaves of circumstance.'

Bird chuckled. 'Crikey, I didn't expect to get a lecture on philosophy and literature when I came here tonight.'

Snow smiled also. 'I wonder what really did bring you here tonight?'

'You mean apart from the taxi …' Bird's eyes twinkled unpleasantly. 'Oh, I just fancied a drink and a chat. I thought you and I bonded in the Indian the other night and maybe we could take it a little further.'

Snow inserted the corkscrew and began turning. 'Bonded?'

'You know … we have things in common.'

'The job?'

'The job, of course … and other things.'

Snow did not respond.

'I mean … we're both bachelors with no ties. A bit lonely. I'm a bit lonely and I reckon you are. Wherever I see you you're on your own. In Sherwood's and the restaurant and the supermarket, shopping for one. Where's the fun in that?'

'It's out of choice,' Snow said, pouring the wine. 'I like it. I am naturally a loner. Police work breeds you that way.'

'Bollocks!'

'Thanks.'

'No offence, but police work binds you together. You need that closeness, the companionship, the camaraderie to get you through the shit we have to deal with. The police is like an extended rather unruly family – unless you're different.'

Snow could see the danger zone on the horizon and was determined to change course. He handed Bird a glass of wine and took a sip from his own.

'What d'you think?'

'Yes, this is good,' he said. 'A Malbec.'

'I know bugger all about wine. I took advice from the guy in the shop and no doubt he was bent on selling me the most expensive bottle on his shelves.'

'Well, it's excellent.'

'Good, well get it down your neck.'

Snow took another sip.

'So, how's the case going? I'm following the progress in the press and colleagues keep passing on little titbits but I don't know the latest.'

'We're getting there, I think. Don't really care to talk shop, I'm afraid.'

'You don't really like to talk about a lot of things, eh, Paul?'

Snow took a small sip of wine. 'I'm a private person, if that's what you mean.'

'Private. Secretive. Deceptive.'

Snow did not respond to this, but already his mind was working on how to get this fellow out of his house before this situation got out of hand.

'Interesting, what you said about Thomas Hardy just now. You know, about free will. "We are not puppets or slaves of circumstance" and all that. I agree, we're not. If we are grown up enough, we should be able make our destinies, make our own choices.'

'Within the bounds of reason and safety.'

'Safety? Surely, we cannot live without risks.'

'Probably not, but we can act to minimise them.'

Bird laughed. 'You're very good, Paul. Very good indeed. But you don't fool me.'

'Have I attempted to fool you?'

Bird drained his glass and placed it at his feet. He leaned forward towards Snow and said in a croaky conspiratorial whisper: 'Sherwood's.'

Again, Snow did not respond.

'You weren't there on a case, were you? Not checking out a suspect, following a line of enquiry? No. You were there as a punter.'

'I was there having a drink.'

'In a gay bar?'

'I was there having a drink.'

'So was I. Having a drink. In a gay bar. I go there quite often. I'm surprised I've not seen you there before.'

'It was my first time. I just wanted a drink.' It was a lie. It sounded like a lie. He knew that Bird would recognise it as such and the only benefit it would serve would be bringing the motive behind his visit out into the open.

'Oh, come now, Paul, don't fib to me. Isn't it time we placed our cards on the table? You know what I'm getting at. You're a bloody good detective, I know that, so don't pretend you don't know what I'm on about.'

'I'm not pretending that, but I am deliberately leaving unspoken that which I don't want to be spoken, to be discussed.'

'Well, hard bloody lines, because I intend to speak about it. You're with a friend here. One who knows. One who is.' Colin Bird winked as he uttered these words.

'I think it's time for you to go now.'

'Only if I get a goodnight kiss.' Bird laughed heartily and then the humour left his face, the features darkening. 'I've been stalking you, you know. It wasn't an accident that I bumped into you in the supermarket this morning. I wanted a romantic tryst, you see.'

Snow rose from his chair and walked to the door and opened it. 'Leave, now, please.'

Bird rose also and beamed at Snow. 'Not such a gallant host then? OK, I will go for now. But I don't intend to leave you alone, Mr Snow. I shall be like a dog with a bone.' As he walked to the outer door, Bird raised his arm with the intention of running his fingers down Snow's cheek but Paul stepped back to avoid contact.

Bird accepted the rebuff with aplomb. 'Next time, eh?' he said, his grin increasing. 'You'll come round, I'm sure. Oh, and don't worry your lovely little head about things: your secret is safe with me.'

After he had gone, Snow wandered back into his sitting room in a kind of daze. He didn't have to ask himself what that was all about, but he did wonder what the hell he was going to do. He opened the sideboard and extracted a bottle of single malt and poured himself a large measure. He put all thoughts on hold until he had taken a generous mouthful. It burnt his throat, warmed his innards and to some extent helped him relax – so much so that he poured himself another.

It would seem, he pondered, as he sipped the whisky with enthusiasm, that he had been propositioned by Colin Bird. He allowed himself a twisted grin as the irony struck him: in the last two days a member of each sex had come on to him. 'I didn't know I was that popular … or versatile,' he muttered to himself with a fey grin, the whisky already helping to slur his words.

Paul Snow woke the following morning with a thick head and a sense of unease. Two paracetemol, a strong coffee and a fierce shower helped to clear his head somewhat, but the feelings of dark anxiety persisted. He had no idea what he was going to do about the Colin Bird situation, but what concerned him all the more was he didn't know what Colin Bird was going to do about him. He remembered snatches of the conversation from the previous evening, particularly Bird's assurance that 'I don't intend to leave you alone, Mr Snow.' As those words echoed in his head, Paul's stomach tightened and he felt queasy.

By the time he reached the office, the habit of focusing on the day's events had helped him shift his concerns regarding Colin Bird to the back of his mind, particularly when he saw a brown envelope on his desk marked 'urgent'. It contained the two photographs taken from the caravan by Sean Quigley of forensics. There was a brief report indicating that there were fingerprints on the pictures but there was no match in the police records.

Snow gazed at the photograph of the girl on her own. She must be a member of the Marsdale Choir, one of those killed in the crash. Somehow he knew that her identity was crucial.

Half an hour later, Snow was parking his car outside Thomas Niven's house in Marsden. It was not quite yet nine o'clock. He hoped the old boy would be up.

He was not only up but was fully dressed and was already tackling the *Daily Telegraph* crossword. Radio Three was playing quietly in the background as Snow was led into the sitting room once more.

'I didn't expect to see you again – or at least so soon,' Niven said, slumping down in his chair. 'What is it this time?'

'I just wondered if you could identify someone for me: the girl in this photograph.' He withdrew the print from the envelope and passed it to Niven, who slipped his gold-rimmed glasses on the end of his nose and studied it.

It did not take him long to respond. 'Why, that's Debbie Hirst. I was telling you about her last time you came. Well, not so much about her, but her mother. You know … she was the one who topped herself by jumping off the bridge on the M62. The grief really got to her. Terrible it was. Mind you, I felt sorry for her husband: to lose both girls, as it were, within a few months. I really don't know how he coped.'

FOURTEEN

Paul Snow and Bob Fellows stood by the gate and stared at the semi-detached house. In many ways, it was no different from the other ordinary properties down this ordinary road. A little shabby, a little mundane, with a garden in need of attention. But there were differences. All the curtains were drawn, both upstairs and down; there were six milk bottles crowding on the front step; some post was seen sticking out of the letterbox; and there was rubbish and debris down the path which had no doubt blown there but had not been removed by the owner. It had all the appearances of being neglected, deserted, abandoned.

As the two policeman made their way down the path, stepping over the detritus and dog dirt, a woman appeared at the front door of the neighbouring property. She was a stout woman in her fifties, wearing a tight grey skirt and an equally tight red sweater which emphasised her generous breasts. No doubt, thought Snow, she thought she looked glamorous rather than blousy.

'You'll get no reply there,' she called. 'He's gone. Done a flit, I should imagine. Haven't seen him in weeks.'

'You are …?' enquired Snow, stepping across the squishy lawn towards the woman. His rather authoritative and educated manner threw the woman for a moment and she stepped back into her hallway. Snow stood by the rickety wooden fence which divided the gardens and held up his ID. 'Police,' he said gently, not wanting to frighten the woman further. 'Mrs? …' he prompted again.

'Fletcher. Is there a problem?'

'Not necessarily,' replied Snow easily. We're just wanting to get in touch with Frank Hirst.'

The woman shook her head vigorously, her straggly hair whipping across her forehead. 'As I said, I ain't seen hide nor hair of him for weeks. And not much before that. He went right into his shell after … you know his wife topped herself, don't you?'

'Yes.'

'And that was after poor Debbie, his daughter, was killed in a crash. A real tragedy.'

Snow nodded.

'It hit him real bad. Could hardly get a "good morning" out of him after. He looked ill, like he needed to see a doctor.'

'How well did you know him?'

Mrs Fletcher screwed up her face. 'Not that much. Just a nodding acquaintance really. I mean we never were in and out of each other's houses or anything like that. I thought she was a bit stuck up, if I'm honest. But we chatted about the weather and such and took in the occasional parcel.'

'When you said that you thought Frank – Mr Hirst – looked like he should seek medical attention, what did you mean exactly?'

Mrs Fletcher thought for a moment, her face twitching as though she was having difficulty marshalling her thoughts. 'It's … it's just something I sensed really,' she said eventually. 'He gave off odd vibes, like. As I say I didn't see much of him after his wife's death but when I did, he looked like a robot, like that Frankenstein monster, walking all stiff and mechanical.' She gave a brief demonstration. 'If I spoke to him, said "Morning" or "How you doing?" it took him ages to reply and then I couldn't quite catch what he was saying. It's as though his brain wasn't quite in gear. I think he was going a bit loopy. To be honest, in the end I avoided him.'

'And you've no idea where he is now?'

Mrs Fletcher shook her head once more, hair flying freely. 'Certainly haven't. I just noticed one day all the curtains drawn and that was it. We stopped the milkman delivering after a week. Has he been up to no good or something?'

'We just want to ask him a few questions.'

'Well, you won't get any answers in there.' She nodded towards the house and then as a thought struck her, she emitted a sharp cry. 'Oh, my God, you don't think he's topped himself, do you? That he's lying dead in there … bloody hell!'

'No, we don't think that. There's no need to get alarmed.'

'Says you,' snapped Mrs Fletcher, hugging herself. 'You don't know for sure.'

Snow decided to direct the conversation away from this particular avenue of thought.

'I don't suppose you have a spare key to the house?'

'No, I don't! Why should I?'

Snow shrugged. 'Sometimes neighbours swap keys – to water plants, feed pets on holidays. Stuff like that.'

'Not us round here. We like to keep our homes private.'

'Well, thanks for your help.' Snow smiled but did not turn to go, keeping his gaze on her until, unnerved by his stare, she retreated into the house, slamming the door behind her.

Bob Fellows chuckled as his boss joined him by the front door.

'Bit of a dragon, eh?' he said, his eyes twinkling with amusement.

'But an informative one. Well, looks like we're going to have to indulge in a little breaking and entering. I think this is where your shoulder comes into its own, Sergeant. If you would be so kind as to apply it to the door with some force.'

'You serious?'

'Do you know any quicker way to gain entry?'

'Maybe not. But why me? You're the senior officer.'

Snow smiled. 'Exactly. That's why I'm giving the orders. Beside, not to put too fine a point on it, you are a bit bulkier than me.'

Bob Fellows grunted. 'Thanks a million.'

Snow stood aside to give his colleague room to make his assault.

Taking a deep breath and moving a few paces back, Bob Fellows hurled himself at the door. It shook but did not give. 'Ouch,' he cried. 'That hurt.'

'You'll get it next time,' said Snow, failing to keep his face completely straight.

Fellows tried again. This time there was the sound of splintering wood, but the door still remained in place. Now Bob tried a different approach. He lifted up his right foot and slammed his size elevens against the lock. This did the trick. The door shuddered, the noise reverberating in the air around them. And then with a sharp crack the door sprang wide open.

Snow patted his sergeant on the back. 'Good man. No one is going to throw sand in your face.'

Bob Fellows rolled his eyes but smiled.

The two men entered the house and immediately their demeanour changed. There was a decided atmosphere which assailed them as soon as they made their way down the hall. The place was cold and there was a faint smell of damp in the air, but it was more than this that contributed to the unpleasantness of the environment. It was also the eerie silence and strange sense of sadness which, although intangible, was experienced by both men. They both shivered involuntarily as they entered the sitting room.

'Crikey,' exclaimed Fellows, gazing around him, 'it looks like he was camping out in his own front room.'

'Indeed,' agreed Snow, surveying the room. There was a little oil stove by the fireplace, around the base of which was a collection of empty cans, mainly soup and baked beans. Dirty plates containing scraps of congealed food and discarded cutlery were scattered around the room, while a sleeping bag lay abandoned on the giant sofa and two full ashtrays were balanced on tiled fender.

'It's as though he couldn't bear to use the rest of the house,' observed Snow.

'Too many memories.'

'Yes. Understandable in one sense, but an extreme reaction nonetheless.'

'Well, if he's the guy we're after, these are the least of his extreme reactions.'

Snow nodded solemnly.

'What do you really think it's all about, sir?'

'I can only surmise but the evidence, which is growing by the day,' he gestured to the shambolic contents of the room, 'suggests that the death of both his daughter and his wife caused Frank Hirst to lose his marbles. In his newly acquired twisted logic, he blames all his ills on the coach crash. He lost his daughter through that and then indirectly his wife. She couldn't face up to life without her precious kid, so she commits suicide. So he has a grudge. A big, all-consuming grudge.'

'Against whom? I mean the logical target would be the driver of the coach. He caused the crash – or that's how it seems, reading between the lines. But he's dead. Who's left to blame?'

Snow shrugged. 'In an unbalanced mind, just about anyone. The chap at the garage who filled the van up with petrol; the people who organised the choir competition in the first place. But he targets … the survivors.'

'What on earth can he blame them for?'

Snow laid a friendly hand on Bob's shoulder. 'For surviving. For escaping the fate that was meted out to his beloved daughter and then to his wife.'

'Really?' The sergeant raised his eyebrows in disbelief. 'That's crazy.'

'Well, that's your theory about murderers, isn't it? No logic involved.'

'Well, yes …'

'But actually, I can see some logic in this plan, if I'm right about the motive, that is. Hirst feels mightily aggrieved. His whole world has collapsed in on him. Who can he blame? Who can he hurt as a kind of revenge? The driver of the coach is dead, so it has to be someone else. Someone to suffer like he has and his two loved ones who have lost their life. And he chooses those that had the luck, the temerity, to survive. Why should they go on living when …?'

'My God! That's awful. It's awful because … well, it is crazy but logical as well. Bloody crazy logic, like.'

'We'll soon know for certain, Bob. We're closing in on him now. Let's take a gander upstairs.'

A thin layer of dust covered everything on the upper floor. Everything was neat and tidy. The beds were made, the towels were carefully folded in the bathroom and clothes hung neatly in the wardrobes. The exception was the little girl's room which was untidy and, apart from the dust, looked as though she had just left it. The covers of the bed were rumpled and some magazines lay on the floor; an LP was on the record player ready to be played. It was a bit like a museum in honour of his daughter, thought Snow.

'It's as though he hasn't actually been up here for ages,' observed Bob as they moved into the main bedroom.

'Since the death of his wife, no doubt. We saw that he had taken to sleeping in the lounge. He obviously neglected this upper storey because it was part of his past. It was filled with too many ghosts. We'd better get the SOCO boys to give this a thorough going over. In the meantime, we need to get a photograph of our Mr Hirst circulated in the press and on the TV. Someone will know where he is. The fellow can't be invisible. Somewhere he is hiding out, planning his next move.'

'He's bound to be getting desperate now, especially as we've got the two girls under surveillance.'

'Too true. That's what worries me. When a cunning violent murderer becomes desperate he takes terrible risks and becomes even more unpredictable.'

FIFTEEN

That night Colin Bird went to Sherwood's again. He was never nervous about his visits. He possessed an arrogance that allowed him to feel protected. If any shit were to hit the fan, he would certainly walk away unscathed. Like Snow, he hid his homosexuality because he wanted to keep his job but in all other respects he was careless. Deliberately so. Normally, when he came to the club, he was on the prowl, ready to pick up someone for the night. He enjoyed sex and he was not too fussy with whom he indulged. Not now, anyway. There had been lots of one-night stands but only one fairly serious affair which had ended unhappily when his partner, Brian, a married man, had committed suicide. For a while, following this tragic event, Bird's world went into freefall. He started drinking and taking up the promiscuous lifestyle. Brian's death had scarred him for life. Never a sentimental nor even a passionate man, he had been surprised how devastated he had been at the loss of Brian. He hadn't realised at the time, not until it was too late, that it had been love: an emotion that had been alien to him. It had scarred him and, although he did not realise it, had unbalanced him also.

And here he was again, feeling something akin to love once more. He had been in the company of Paul Snow just a few hours, but he knew that he was the man for him. It certainly helped that he not only looked a little like Brian but also had that same gentle sense of reserve and enticing smile, when he could be coaxed into showing it. The fact that he was playing hard to get increased his attraction.

Colin had not come to Sherwood's tonight for a pick-up. He just wanted to be with his own kind, so that he could brood. Think about Paul Snow. Think how he could win him over. Coax the lovely bastard out of his shell. Well, it wasn't so much a shell as a straitjacket – as he'd told him. They could be good together, mused Bird, as he sipped his gin and tonic, if only Paul would be true to his feelings. The more he drank, the more the fire of determination grew within him. He was not going to be fobbed off. He had lost Brian but he was not going to lose Paul. He would break the fellow down or else he would break the fellow. Whatever he had to do, he would do it to bring about what he wanted. In the mind of this lonely and somewhat disturbed man, the obsession, which only a few days previously had been but a seed, flourished with grotesque growth.

It was while he was on his fourth gin and tonic that a middle-aged man in a double-breasted suit, wearing some kind of club tie, slipped into the chair beside him.

'Hello, there, chummy,' he said, his hand slithering over the table to touch Colin's. 'Been watching you for a while. Thought you needed cheering up. I reckon I might be the fellow to do it.'

Colin gazed for some moments at the stranger before responding. When he did, he spat the words out with vehemence: 'Piss off, you queer bastard,' he said.

Eva Hodge poured herself another generous measure of sherry – up to the brim – and lit up a cigarette. This, along with the telly, was her usual evening's entertainment. Since her husband had done a bunk with that belly dancer, her life had been dedicated to her little boarding house, business and fags and a few sherries in the evening. As she confided to her neighbour Andrea, actually she got more bodily sensation from a couple of ciggies and several swigs from the cream sherry bottle than she ever did from her ex. Of course, she knew there were a few things missing from her life, but she was happy that one of them was Dennis.

She laid back on the couch and split open a pack of Maltesers. Why not? She knew she had a fat stomach and a saggy bum, but what the hell. At fifty-five the days of trying to lure a bloke to her bed were well over. At her age there were more important appetites. She intended to treat herself, indulge herself until she keeled over in the drinks aisle at the supermarket. The rather dreary drama on TV came to a close as she crunched her last Malteser. Time for bed, she thought. I'll just watch the late local news and then beddy byes. With some difficulty she pulled herself up in readiness for padding off to her bedroom. The news was as dreary as the drama until something appeared on screen which made her heart jump and her stomach retch. Her chubby fingers reached for the remote control to increase the volume.

There on her television was the face of her new lodger. The version that stared out at her from the screen was clean-shaven and well groomed, the eyes bright with the mouth bearing a natural smile. He was a far cry from the shifty bearded scruff she had just let her spare room to but nevertheless it was the same man. She was sure of it. She only caught the details about the police wanting to interview him. The newsreader quickly moved on to some local football results.

Eva Hodge froze for a moment, her vision blurring and the sound of the television fading to a faint mumble.

'... the police wanting to interview him ...' Why? What had he done? Was he a rapist? A murderer? Whatever, he was a bloody wrong 'un and he was staying in her house. Christ almighty! At this thought she began to gag and felt her bladder loosen. My God, what was she to do? He might come in at any time and do her in. In desperation she pulled herself to her feet and staggered to the door, the intake of sherry making the room shimmer somewhat. She couldn't lock herself in because there was no lock on the door to her sitting room. She looked around in befuddled desperation. Her eyes lit upon the armchair. With great effort Eva swung the chair round and rammed it up against the door. In reality she knew that it wouldn't keep a determined brutish rapist out but it gave her a little comfort.

The fear she felt building up inside her helped to clear her mind and she grabbed the phone. She had to ring the police. Words came awkwardly at first: her mouth was dry and the sherry was still slurring her speech. She hoped to God that the coppers didn't think this was a hoax call or just some drunk off her head.

'That man on the telly that the police want,' she said, desperately trying to articulate each word. 'He's here. In my house. I saw his picture on the telly. He's ... got a beard now but it's him. I know it's him. He's here in my house. He could kill me. You've got to come and help. Please.'

The voice at the other end asked for details, including Eva's address.

'Keep calm,' the voice said. 'Someone will be with you shortly.'

'Thank God.' Eva replaced the receiver and slumped back on the sofa, tears misting her eyes. She caught sight of the sherry bottle and her hand instinctively reached out for it, but as her fingers clasped the cold glass of the neck, she stopped. Better not, she thought. I need to stay sober. Warily she glanced over to the door and its rather insubstantial barrier, while she hugged herself tightly.

Snow was already in bed when he received the call, but so practised and disciplined was he in matters of getting himself dressed and out of the house at speed that he was turning the ignition of his car ready to set off within five minutes of replacing the receiver.

Eva Hodge's house was in Berry Rise, the Farwell area of Huddersfield, one of the shabbier locales in the town. It had quite a high crime rate, drugs and prostitution mainly, but it had been the scene of a couple of rather nasty knife attacks, gang related, in the last couple of years. It didn't take Snow long to locate Berry Rise. There was already a police car with a flashing light parked outside. Apparently the mainstream plods had never heard of the softly, softly catchee monkee approach. Just dive in there with as much illumination and noise as possible, announce your presence to all and sundry, including the guy you are attempting to apprehend. One sight of the flashing blue light and he would have high-tailed for the hills.

There was a burly copper on the door. Paul was about to retrieve his ID but the constable recognised him.

'Evening, sir.'

Snow nodded and entered the property. He made a left and turned into the main room, where two uniformed officers, one male and female, were talking to a blousy middle-aged woman who was clasping a small tumbler containing a brown fluid. Brandy, whisky or maybe sherry, Snow guessed. She looked distressed, flushed and a little drunk.

'DI Snow,' Paul announced himself, more to the officers, than to the woman.

'DS Scott, sir, and this is DS Perkins.'

'So, what is the situation?'

'The man's not here. His room is empty.'

'The man's not here, and he's unlikely to return, seeing that there's a police car with flashing lights outside,' observed Snow, coldly.

'Here, you, don't get narky with these two,' growled Eva Hodge, shuffling herself forward on the sofa, her bleary eyes flashing with annoyance. 'They've saved my bacon. I don't want that scumbag to come back. I don't want him anywhere near this place. I could have been murdered in my bed if these two hadn't turned up to rescue me.'

'Of course,' said Snow diplomatically. It would be dangerous to rub the old soak up the wrong way. He could see that alcohol was already making her irrational. He didn't want to exacerbate her condition by aggravating her. 'You were very wise to give us a call. You saw the picture on the television news, I gather.'

Eva Hodge nodded. 'Gave me the fright of my life. Staring out at me. Like a bloody bogey man. I should have trusted my instincts and turned the bastard away. I felt he was a wrong 'un in me waters.'

'How long has he been your … paying guest?'

'Only just a few days. I usually have such smart gentle-men. He was rather rough looking, but he was quiet and paid me up front. Mind you, if I'd known … What's the bastard done?'

'We just need to talk to him, to help us with our enquiries.'

'Enquiries about what?'

'When did you last see him?'

Eva Hodge screwed up her face. 'Can't rightly say. As I say, he's very quiet. I'll give him that. Hardly know he's around. This morning. I think. Yes … that's right. I caught sight of him as he left.'

'Does he have a car – or a van?'

'I don't know. There's nothing parked outside.'

'What name did he give you?'

'Black, Jim Black. But that's not his real name, is it?'

'Would you mind showing us his room?'

With some effort, Eva Hodge raised herself from the sofa and made her way to the sideboard. Opening a drawer, she extracted a bunch of keys.

'This way,' she said, beckoning to Snow.

'You two wait here,' he told the two officers softly and followed the woman out of the door.

The room in which Eva Hodge's 'paying guest' had stayed was basic in the extreme. A naked sixty-watt bulb illuminated the contents in harsh relief. There was a bed, a cheap wardrobe and chest of drawers, and a bedside cabinet topped by a small lamp. Snow dropped down on the floor and checked under the bed. There was a prodigious amount of grey fluff but nothing else. A small holdall dumped by the bed attracted his attention, but on examination it only contained a couple of shirts, some socks and two pairs of underpants. There was nothing else in the room. The drawers and wardrobe were empty. Frank Hirst travelled extremely light, leaving no significant mark. He was a clever and cautious man.

Snow reckoned that his other stuff must be housed in his van, for surely he would have acquired another vehicle. This was a necessity for his mission. He would most likely park it nearby but not where it could be seen from of the house so that Mrs Hodge wouldn't catch sight of it.

Snow gave the room one final perusal. He would get the SOCO team in there, but he was fairly sure that they would not come up with anything apart from some patches of mould and the odd bed bug or two. Certainly nothing that would further the investigation.

'The room is off limits for now, Mrs Hodge, until the technical chaps have gone over it looking for clues,' he said as pleasantly as he could, fully aware that Mrs Hodge did not care for him at all.

'They're welcome to it. But am I safe here? What if he comes back and tries to kill me?'

Snow shook his head. 'There's no danger of that, but I'll get one of the officers to stay with you overnight to make sure you're safe.'

She shuddered. 'I should have never let the bugger in. I should have relied on my instincts. They told me he was a wrong 'un.'

As they moved on to the landing, she turned the switch, plunging the room into stygian darkness.

SIXTEEN

'Did you always want to be a policewoman?' Elizabeth Saunders played with her hair absent-mindedly as she sat on her bed opposite WPC Angela Dawes.

'I think so,' the officer replied gently. 'It's good to help people.'

Elizabeth thought for a moment. 'I think I'd like to be one, too. Is it difficult?'

Angela smiled. 'If I can do it, I'm sure you can. You have to be dedicated and put a lot of effort into training, but if you are determined, you will make it.'

Elizabeth pulled a wisp of hair towards her mouth. 'I bet it's exciting. Do you get to catch a lot of criminals?'

'I think that's enough questions for tonight,' observed Elizabeth's mother, who had been sitting in the shadows at the far side of the bedroom.

'Oh, Mum, not yet.'

'Oh, yes, it's late and you have school in the morning.'

PC Dawes nodded. 'Your mum's right. If you want to be a policewoman, you've got to get a good education and you need to be bright and bushy-tailed for school.'

Elizabeth sighed and pouted her lips. 'OK.'

'Good girl,' said PC Dawes, touching the little girl gently on the shoulder.

'Thanks very much,' said her mother. 'I'll take it from here.'

Angela nodded. 'She'll be safe for the night now. I'll wait downstairs for a while before getting off.'

Mrs Saunders gave a strained smile, stress clearly etched on her pale features. As a single mother, the burden of the last few days had worn her down. The police had been reasonably circumspect as to the extent of the danger that her daughter was in but, as a sensitive, intelligent woman, she had realised it must be pretty serious for them to give her daughter twenty-four-hour protection. 'Thank you. Thank you for all your help. It's a comfort to know you're around.'

'No problem,' said Angela, leaving the room to allow mother and daughter some moments of privacy and intimacy before the little girl settled down to sleep. All she had to do now was wait downstairs in the kitchen until ten o'clock when she would be relieved by another officer.

Upstairs, Mrs Saunders was sitting on the bed, stroking her daughter's forehead as the little girl snuggled down under the covers.

'It's nice having a policewoman in the house, isn't it, Mum?' the girl said sleepily.

'You get a good night's sleep, darling,' replied her mother, avoiding the issue. 'No bad dreams, eh?'

'No.' Her little mouth opened in a gentle yawn and the eyelids fluttered momentarily before closing.

Mrs Saunders waited a few moments, watching her daughter with love and apprehension as she drifted off to sleep. How could anyone try to hurt such an innocent little thing? At this thought, tears pricked at her eyes and she felt her chest heave. No, no, she told herself. She must not cry. She must not give into emotion. She had to be strong. Stoical should be her watchword. Nothing – nothing – was going to happen to her lovely daughter.

Nothing.

Leaving the pink nightlight on, Mrs Saunders went downstairs.

Across the road, standing in the shadows under a tree, was a dark figure who was staring at the house, his eyes caught particularly by the soft glow from one of the upstairs bedrooms. That must be the little girl's room, he reckoned. That was his challenge. He knew there was a police officer inside the house as well as the girl's mother. Those were the two obstacles he had to overcome. Stepping out of the shadows, he crossed the road, his eyes focused on the house as he tried to work out how he could gain access to the property and then ensure his escape. Was it impossible? Maybe. But he couldn't fail in his mission at this late stage. He didn't really want anyone else to get hurt – just the child. Just the survivor. He shook his head. As he approached the house, he saw how impossible a task it was. He could easily gain entry, but how was he to snatch the child and escape with her? Get her to his van. Well, he couldn't, could he? He would have to re-think. It had to be at the school. He would have to snatch her at the school. Somehow. Some way. He had to do it there.

He pulled the van on to the waste ground, several streets away from his lodgings. He groaned with misery at his lack of progress, his body slumping over the wheel. Things were getting really difficult now and he knew the police were closing in on him. He could feel their presence like a rough noose slowly tightening around his neck. It had been so easy at the start but now there were so many obstacles. It had been a fairly straight road down which he'd travelled, but now this pathway had turned into a maze of cruel complexity.

He didn't mind being caught when it was all over – in fact he welcomed being caught then, for there would be nothing else left for him. He would be happy to spend the rest of his days staring at the grey walls of a cell, knowing he had righted a great wrong, that he had carried out acts of justice in honour of his little girl. But to be apprehended before he had finished what he had set out to do would be a tragedy. The thought of this turned his stomach and tears began to stream down his face. More and more now, unbidden and unfettered emotion would overtake him without warning, shaking his body and causing a harsh tightness across the chest. He did not fight it. He allowed this strange passionate reaction to have its way with his body. He now considered it almost a cleansing process, as though the tears and the pain were exorcising his fears and doubts. After a few minutes, the tremors and tears subsided, leaving his body limp and his mind exhausted. He lay for quite a while resting across the wheel of the van, neither fully awake nor asleep, a kind of ease restoring itself.

At length he pulled himself up, dragged the sleeve of his coat across his face to catch some of the dampness there and then got out of the vehicle. Tomorrow is another day, he told himself, the cliché rebuilding his strength of purpose. He would act tomorrow, whatever. That girl would die tomorrow. With this thought firmly in mind, buoying up his spirits, he set off towards Eva Hodge's guest house and a good night's rest.

However, when he turned the corner of the street, a shock was in store for him. Parked outside Mrs Hodge's house was a police car, garish and shiny, illuminated by the fierce amber glow of the street light. He froze for a moment taking in the scene and then instinctively he stepped backwards into the shadows, his horrified eyes never leaving the offensive vehicle for a second.

'What the fuck,' he mouthed as a faint whisper. They were on to him. But how? Well, the how didn't really matter. What really mattered was that there was a police car outside the place where he had been kipping and no doubt there was a burly copper inside the house at this very moment, turning over his room looking for clues. That phrase caused him to give a twisted grin. It wasn't 'his room' for Christ's sake, it was just the place where he had hoped to hole up for a few days. Thank God, he had kept the stuff he'd taken in there to a minimum. But, nevertheless … they were that close to him.

Amid these thoughts, the question came again: how? How had the police found out where he was staying? What had he done wrong? How had he slipped up? God, he had to get the hell away from here. And fast.

In an instant he was running, running as fast as he could back to the van. Within minutes he was revving up the engine and the wheels where churning up the mud on the waste ground as the vehicle rocked and lurched forward. With a swaying motion, it bumped on to the road and it turned left away from Mortar Street and Mrs Eva Hodge's place. Frank Hirst wasn't conscious of the red Cavalier speeding past him in the opposite direction, the driver, his lean pallid face drawn in concentration. Equally, Detective Inspector Paul Snow had no notion that he had just driven past the man he was seeking, the murderer of three young girls.

SEVENTEEN

It was half past midnight when Paul Snow eventually made his way home. As he drove away from Mortar Street he tried to assess objectively whether tonight's surprise event had actually benefited the investigation or not. It was a close call. In one sense the net was closing in on Frank Hirst, but while they had sealed off one of his hidey holes, they had done it in such a fashion as to alert him to how close they were on his tail and, like a cunning, frightened mole, he would burrow a great deal deeper now and take more precautions. It was almost a guerrilla war scenario. They knew where he was likely to strike – or try to strike – but how he would do it and when were still questions for which they had no answers. Snow believed that Hirst was so dedicated in his mission to kill all those who had survived his own daughter, and only those, that he would not harm anyone else in his attempt to bring this to a successful conclusion. To kill or even injure someone whom Hirst would see as an innocent bystander would contaminate the purity of his cause. It had to be those who had cheated death. And only those. That was how Snow viewed it. He couldn't be sure he was right or that Bob Fellows and his other colleagues would see it in the same light.

One thing was for sure. He had to organise tighter security for the two girls tomorrow. They were in greater danger than ever now. Bloody hell, he thought as he put his key into the lock, it already is tomorrow. He checked his wrist watch. It was 12.45. So much for my early night.

He turned the key but the door wouldn't open. Wait a minute, he thought, I moved the key to the right. That would have locked the door. To test this theory, he twisted the key in the opposite direction and the door opened. Don't tell me that I left in such a hurry that I forgot to lock the door. Snow cast his mind back to his departure earlier that night. He had a vision of himself locking the door. He was very particular about his own security. But was that a true vision or wishful thinking? He groaned quietly. He really was too tired to work it out but still a feeling of unease settled on him as he entered his sitting room.

As he did so, the table lamp in the corner clicked on, filling the room with a pale yellow light, by which Snow observed a figure sitting in the armchair by the fire.

'What time do you call this?' the figure said, leaning forward so that Snow could see his face. He had already recognised the voice before he caught sight of the features in the lamp's glow.

It was Colin Bird.

'What the hell are you doing here?' he asked, his voice bristling with anger.

'I've come to see you.'

'How … how the hell did you get in?'

'Oh, come now. I'm a policeman. I have my methods.'

Snow's instinct was to grab the bastard by the throat and thump him hard, but despite being weary and angry he was sharp enough to realise that he may well come off the worse in such an encounter. Bird was taller and of a larger build than him. A different tactic was needed. With a swift movement, Snow returned to the door and switched the main light on, blinking as the shadows vanished in the harsh illumination.

'Would you like to tell me what this is all about?' He had tried to adopt a reasonable tone but he failed to keep the anger out of his voice.

Bird flashed him a smile. 'It's about you. It's about you, Paul Snow. I wanted to see you.'

Snow shook his head. 'You're not making sense. You're saying you broke into my house, the home of a fellow police officer, because you wanted to see me. That just doesn't make fucking sense!'

'It does to me, Paul. You must know that I have feelings for you.'

'Feelings.' A ghost walked over Paul Snow's grave.

Bird rose from the chair. He was no longer smiling. His face now wore a pale mask of anguish. 'Feelings. Yes, I love you.'

'What!' Snow shook his head in disbelief. Was this tragi-comedy really being played out in his living room?

'I know you share the same feelings as me,' Bird was saying, 'it's just that you won't admit them.'

'Don't be ridiculous. I don't feel anything for you.'

'Are you denying you're gay?'

Oh, my God, thought Paul, not this again. He shook his head. 'Yes, I am denying it.'

'You bloody liar. No straight man goes to Sherwood's. I know that. You've been there more than once. I made enquiries. And don't come up with some cock and bull story about being on a case or carrying out some sur-veillance because I've checked up on you, DI Paul Snow.'

Snow paused. This was getting deep now and seri-ous. Was he really in danger of his secret being exposed? How indiscreet had Bird been in his enquiries? The stupid bastard. Snow thought again: was Colin Bird just an infatuated fool or, indeed, was this a honey trap?

'You are deluded, Colin, and you are acting in a dan-gerous and irresponsible fashion. Breaking and entering is a serious offence.'

'But you won't report me, will you, Paul? To do that would mean questions, awkward questions would be asked and maybe the truth would come out.'

'The truth?'

'About you. About you being a closet queer.'

Now Paul really wanted to smash Bird in the face. In essence he was threatening to expose him and to ruin his career. And what for? Some misguided, irrational crush he seemed to have on him. It was clear that Bird had no concerns about his sexuality being revealed and equally had no qualms about dragging Snow into the limelight along with him.

'You are mistaken, Colin, and rather disturbed,' Snow said evenly. 'You have misread so much. You have to pack up these thoughts and discard them. Go home and get some rest. Take a few days' leave. I won't say a thing about this episode, but you have to forget about it. And forget about me. I don't want to see you again or have you making any attempt to contact me.'

Bird gave a mirthless laugh. 'Are you so much of a coward? You cannot admit to me in the privacy of your own home where your feelings lie?'

'They certainly do not lie with you.'

'They might, if you gave them a chance. I'm a very caring person, Paul. We could be good together.'

Paul shook his head. 'This is madness.'

'The only madness is your denial. You need to stagger out into the daylight and release your inner passion. It's not wrong, you know. It's only other people who say it is. People who have no idea.'

'I have no inner passion like yours.' The words came thickly. Paul hated himself for uttering them. They were a lie and in making such a claim he was committing an act of self-betrayal. But he had no alternative. Long ago he had sworn never to leave that very restrictive closet into which he'd been born. Homosexuals were either pilloried or parodied and shunted to the periphery of society. They were viewed as the unclean by the general public at large. The press and media presented them as mincing clowns or evil sex fiends. Anyone who was of that persuasion in a position of authority from bank managers to politicians to magistrates was fair game for blackmail, exposure and trashing in the press. Great delight was expressed when outing and destroying the career of the closet gay. Snow should know. He had been the victim of blackmail and he vowed it would never happen again.

'How can you say that?' Bird said, rising from the chair. 'It is a lie. You know it is a lie. We can share the secret together. I am not here to harm you. I am here to love you.'

Paul took a step back. His mind was a whirl. His usually self-contained nature, precise and practical, was thrown into confusion. He had no ideas, plans or procedures for such a situation. Not only was it unique but it had very dark and far-reaching connotations. He found himself saying, 'Don't be ridiculous.'

'Oh, Paul, it is you who is being ridiculous. If you would just let your guard down, think what wonderful things you could experience: real companionship, love and sex.'

'Get it into your head, I have no feelings for you. No feelings!' Snow was shouting now and the words echoed round the room.

Bird took a step forward. 'Give it a chance. I know deep down that you want to.'

Paul gave out an exasperated groan. 'Just go, will you.'

'Not until you admit to me …'

'I will admit nothing. This is crazy talk.'

Bird grabbed hold of Snow's arms and thrust his face so close, he could feel the warm breath on his cheek.

'I don't want to hurt you or upset you. Can't you see that I care about you?' He leaned forward and to Snow's horror he realised that the man was going to kiss him. There was something now in Bird's features, particularly his eyes, that Snow noticed for the first time. Perhaps it was only being exhibited for the first time. It was madness. Snow had seen it in the eyes of criminals. That slightly wild glassiness in the pupils that indicated that the person had lost touch with reality and was inhabiting his own twisted world. Whatever they were doing, no matter how wrong it was, they believed it was right. Bird had that same look. The man had lost it.

Snow acted quickly. With a powerful jerk of his arms, he thrust Bird away from him. The action was so violent that Bird fell backwards, knocking the armchair sideways in his fall, landing flat on his back on the carpet with a gasp of surprise. For some seconds both men remained still, as though they were appearing in a film that had been freeze framed. In reality they were each held by the bizarre nature of the events that had just unfolded: events that were both tragic and farcical. They had shifted into surreal territory. After a few moments Paul moved forward and extended his hand in an offer to help Bird up from his prone position. The offer was refused with a vicious swipe of the hand and a snarl.

'You bastard,' Bird roared, dragging himself to his feet. His whole demeanour had changed now. The shoulders were hunched aggressively and his features seemed to bloat with anger. 'You're going to regret this, you spineless bastard,' he said, the voice a subterranean growl. 'I've gone out on a limb coming to you like this and you just kick me in the teeth. I express my feelings for you and in return you attack me …'

Snow shook his head vigorously. 'I didn't attack you … I was trying to stop you doing something stupid. Look, I'm sorry you feel this way but you have misread the whole scenario.'

'Have I? Have I really? So you're not gay. You're not shit scared that you'll be ousted as PC Pansy and you've not just spit in my face …'

Snow was at a loss for words. He knew that whatever he said would only fuel Bird's anger. He just shrugged his shoulders and sighed wearily.

'I don't take rejection well, Paul. Not well at all,' said Bird, making for the door.

'It's not rejection … it's just that you're misreading the signs.'

'That's fucking rubbish and you know it. You might fool yourself but you don't fool me. This isn't over yet, I can tell you.' He walked out of the room, slamming the door.

Snow slumped down on to the sofa. He was emotionally drained and deeply depressed. 'Oh, Lord,' he murmured to himself, 'what the hell's going to happen now?' He let his head fall into his hands, the palms blanking his vision. He stayed like that for nearly ten minutes without moving. Eventually, he rose somewhat mechanically and made his way into the kitchen. Extracting a bottle of whisky from one of the cupboards, he poured himself a large one. As he took a gulp, he remembered what his father used to say when he had an occasional nip: 'For medicinal purposes only, you realise.' He smiled at the memory and uttered the words aloud to himself. Well, he thought, as he took another drink, he hoped that it would act as an effective sleeping draught yet again. After the day he'd had, he desperately needed a good night's sleep.

EIGHTEEN

Dawn was just asserting itself in the leaden skies over Huddersfield as Frank Hirst shuffled wearily into a greasy spoon up by the bus station. He was depressed and very hungry. He ordered a cup of tea and a bacon sandwich from the bleary-eyed girl serving. She wasn't fully awake yet and was functioning on automatic pilot. It was lucky for Hirst that she was, for she hardly gave him a glance as she attended to his order in clumsy silence.

Moving to a table near the door, Hirst took a satisfying gulp of the scalding tea. Its ferocity helped to shake off some of the malaise that had settled upon him through lack of sleep and worry. Then came the delight of the bacon sandwich, enhanced by a blob of brown sauce squeezed with a farting noise from a plastic container.

The previous occupant of the table had left a morning newspaper behind and Hirst, almost out of a sense of habit, pulled it towards him and began idly to turn the pages while he continued to chew on the bacon sandwich. He froze mid-bite when his eyes fell upon a picture on one of the inside pages. It was a photograph of a face well known to him. It was his own. The text was short and to the point. This man was wanted by the police to help them with their enquiries. He was not to be approached as he could be dangerous. There was a dedicated telephone number to ring to report any sightings.

Instinctively Hirst gazed round him, eyeing the other customers in the café to see if they were about to point a finger at him or rush out to the nearest phone box and ring that dedicated number. There were four other customers, each sitting on their own, each hunched up over their mugs of tea or coffee, each lost in their own morning thoughts. It was zombie-land.

Hirst returned his scrutiny to the picture once more. Here he was in the good old days. Bright-eyed, clean shaven, short tidy hair, wearing a collar and tie. A million miles from the wreck that he now was. Hair over his ears, a grey straggly beard, grubby features, sallow skin, and wearing a greasy anorak. He was a different person. Both outside and in.

However, the photograph in the paper confirmed that now the police had put the pieces of the puzzle together and they knew who he was and what he was about. They were closing in on him with a rapidity that unnerved him. There was absolutely no time to lose. He still had two tasks to complete. He would, he realised, have to be more reckless now than ever. And if that meant others got hurt in the process – so be it.

'Come on, love, get your breakfast eaten before it goes cold.' Mrs Hargreaves stood behind her son and placed her hands on his shoulders, giving them a gentle, affectionate shake.

'I'm not really hungry, Mum,' he said.

'Oh, come on now, Alan, you're not still dwelling on that bloke what got away, are you?'

PC Alan Hargreaves swivelled around in his chair to face his mother, his features clouded with misery. 'It was my fault he escaped. What kind of a copper am I if I let a bloody child-killer get away? You can imagine what they're saying about me down at HQ.'

'No, I can't and neither can you. If they're decent folk they'll know you did your best.'

'Yeah and my best isn't good enough.'

'Nonsense. You were bright enough to spot the van in the first place. If it wasn't for you they wouldn't have that as evidence. You don't know what kind of help that might be to them. And that's all because of you.'

Hargreaves did not reply but looked far from convinced by his mother's argument.

'Now come on, Alan, get that breakfast down you. You don't want to be feeling faint when you're on the road, do you? You're in a patrol car today, aren't you?

Alan Hargreaves nodded, turned reluctantly and in a desultory fashion began to eat his bacon and egg.

It was while he was cleaning his teeth that the idea came to him. It formed quickly and he resolved to act upon it. Since his failure to apprehend 'the man in the van', he had taken pains to find out more details concerning the case and to read up what notes were available to him as a lowly constable, one who was not qualified enough yet to be part of any investigative team. It had helped him form a general picture of the situation. He was aware that there were now two young girls under police protection and they were the vulnerable ones. He had made a note of their addresses and the schools which they attended. The more he had mulled these facts over, he believed that the killer had a restricted opportunity to strike – an opportunity he would be desperate to take.

Two girls. Which one deserved his attention? He just had to choose one like the fall of a dice. He decided on Elizabeth Saunders simply because he liked the name Elizabeth. He knew that she attended St Jude's Catholic School in the Almondbury district and that she would be taken to the school by WPC Jean Fraser. It wouldn't do any harm to observe them. Who knew what he might see?

Hirst got into the school early. It was so easy. Only the cleaners were about and he easily avoided those. Presumably the caretaker was somewhere to be found on the premises but Hirst saw neither hide nor hair of him. He couldn't believe his luck. With surreptitious movement down the various poorly lit corridors – not fully illuminated until the teachers and students arrived – he familiarised himself with the layout of the school on the ground floor. He was particularly interested in the head teacher's study and the various rooms close by. In closely inspecting this corridor he discovered exactly what would suit his purposes. A walk-in kind of broom cupboard. It was unlocked and looked neglected. The gods were smiling on him today.

At first Elizabeth Saunders had enjoyed the attention and celebrity that being accompanied by a policewoman to school had brought her. It had marked her out as special. Rather like a pop star attending a concert and being protected by security guards. And she quite liked her official chaperones, especially WPC Fraser – 'call me Jeannie'. She had a kind, mumsy way with her and smelt nice. But after a few days the novelty wore off. She found that when she arrived at school and Jeannie stayed with her in the playground until the bell went for registration, her friends tended to avoid her, not wanting to mix with a grown-up in uniform. Elizabeth felt isolated. And she had run out of conversation with Jeannie. She wanted to chat with her mates about school, boys and other girlie things – topics that she couldn't talk to Jeannie about.

WPC Fraser had sensed this change and if the truth be known she was rather bored with this particular chore and was relieved when the bell rang and the girls began to troop inside the school and her duties were over for that morning.

'Look after yourself. Take care and I'll see you this afternoon,' she said, smoothing Elizabeth's hair in an affectionate manner.

The girl nodded, her eyes already seeking out her friends. 'Thanks,' she muttered as she skipped off quickly to join the throng of girls entering the school.

WPC Jeannie Fraser sighed. She wondered how long this was going to last. She hadn't joined the police force to become a superannuated nanny. Heading back to the car, she had visions of a hot cup of tea and a fag waiting for her back at the canteen. As she slipped into the patrol car, she took no notice of a shabby blue van parked across the road from the entrance to the school. Slipping a mint in her mouth, she drove off at speed.

As Elizabeth made her way down the crowded corridor in haste, attempting to catch up with a couple of her friends, she felt a tug on her satchel. Turning, she discovered a shadowy figure facing her. It was a man of medium height. He wore a long raincoat and some kind of cap on his head, with the brim pulled well forward over his eyes. His chin was adorned by a rather scruffy beard and he was carrying a very large sports bag.

'Sorry to bother you, miss,' he said in a quiet, polite voice, 'I'm lost. Can you show me to the head's office? I have an appointment with her, you see.'

Elizabeth hesitated. She really wanted to see her friends before registration took place. For this procedure, Mr Maynard, her form teacher, demanded silence while he filled in the ticks and crosses with neat precision, so there was no chance of a gossip then. However, she knew that it would be rude to refuse this request from a visitor to the school. They had all been drilled about behaving politely to strangers.

'It's down the other way. I'll show you. Follow me.'

'Thank you, miss,' said the man.

Moving against the tide of youngsters, Elizabeth led the man back towards the main foyer and then along a side corridor.

'It's down there on the right,' she said, pointing.

The man smiled strangely. 'Where exactly? Would you show me?'

The girl raised her eyebrows in frustration. How thick was this chap? The room had a sign on it saying 'Head teacher'. A kid of five could find it.

Without a word and stifling an irritated sigh, she walked down the corridor. There was no one else in sight. As they neared the head teacher's room, she thought the man behind her faltered, but before she was able to turn round, she felt a pad of something soft clamped to her mouth and a strong arm around her neck. She tried to call out, to scream, but she couldn't. Soon she lost the power to struggle as the fumes from the cloth held firmly against her face assailed her senses. A ferocious drowsiness overpowered the girl and her limbs began to turn to jelly as she lost consciousness.

In an instant, Hirst had dragged the girl into the nearby broom cupboard. He laid her gently on the floor and gazed with rapt attention at her inert form. For a fleeting moment he was tempted to complete the deed here and now. However, no matter how tempting that was, it had not been part of his plan and he quickly swept this notion aside. To act impulsively was too dangerous and besides he wanted the satisfaction of leaving the body in a more appropriate location. He must stick to his original plan.

He laid the large sports bag on the floor by the girl and unzipped it. Gently, he folded her body, bringing her knees up to her stomach and lowering her head on to her chest. Then he lifted the girl and placed her body inside the bag. He brushed her hair down over her face so that it would not be caught in the zip. Once, she was neatly encased inside the bag, he fastened it. He paused for a few moments, taking a series of deep breaths before opening the door of the small room and gazing out into the corridor. A young girl scurried past and disappeared, and then the coast was clear. Hauling up the bag which now sagged with its new contents, he stepped out into the corridor and, with as much haste as possible, he made his way towards the exit.

PC Alan Hargreaves had been parked up a narrow side street just opposite St Jude's Catholic School for some time and he had a clear view of the entrance. He was in an unmarked patrol car – a black Vauxhall Corsa. He was due to be up touring the Ainley Top stretch of the M62 motorway on the lookout for speeders, but he just wanted to check out his hunch first of all. He knew he was taking a risk and he certainly would be for the high jump if he was found out, but he knew he just had to take the risk. After all, effective policing inevitably involved taking chances.

He was there before WPC Jean Fraser had arrived with the young girl, Elizabeth Saunders, but not before Frank Hirst had entered the school premises. He watched all the arrivals at the school assiduously, noting everyone who had entered the gates. Some of the students had been accompanied by parents, some arriving in cars while a whole troop disembarked from a double-decker bus, swarming noisily through the gates. He could see the small staff car park from his vantage point and had observed all those parking there. None of the adults bore any resemblance to the suspect, the scruffy bearded man he had nearly apprehended. By now the front of the school was quiet. All the inmates, it seemed, were inside for the day.

Well, he mused sadly, the whole idea had been a grasping at straws exercise anyway. With a sigh, he accepted that in his heart of hearts, he didn't think that the murderer would turn up in broad daylight and attempt to snatch the girl, no matter how twisted his mind was now. He was about to turn the key in the ignition when he saw a figure emerge from the front of the school. It was a fellow in a long raincoat and tweed flat cap, pulled well down over his forehead. He hadn't see him before. He was carrying a very large sports bag which from the fellow's gait and stooped posture was extremely heavy indeed.

PC Hargreaves wound down his window and leaned out to get a clearer view of this man. He stared hard, trying to get a good look at his features, which were difficult to see because he kept his head thrust down on his chin in the shadow of his cap.

There was something about his demeanour and that oddly shaped, heavy sports bag which prompted a series of prickling sensations at the back of PC Hargreaves' neck. As a policeman he was trained to view most things as potentially suspicious, but in this case he was fairly convinced there was something that was not quite right. As the man reached the kerbside, he raised his head to check that it was safe to cross, and as he did so, Hargreaves caught sight of his face – the face and that scruffy beard. The prickling sensations went off the Richter scale. This was the man. This was the bloody man.

Christ!

He was already across the road and stowing the sports bag into the back of a grey van, not unlike the other one he had encountered. What should he do now, thought Hargreaves. If he got out of his car and tried to apprehend the man, by the time he had reached the vehicle, he would have had time to drive off. No, it would be best if he followed him. See where the bastard was going. One horrific thought struck him as he started up the engine. That sports bag. That heavy, distended sports bag. What on earth did it contain? PC Hargreaves' stomach flipped as he answered his own question.

NINETEEN

Paul Snow had arrived late at the office that morning. This was partly because he had slept very badly, thanks to Colin Bird's visit the previous night, and partly because he was suffering from a mild hangover after indulging too much in the malt whisky into the early hours. He was angry with himself for this. He knew that while alcohol may deaden sensations and concerns temporarily, it does not alter circumstances or provide any solutions. After issuing a few gruff 'good mornings', he had hidden himself away in his office, where he dosed himself with several black coffees. He hoped that he wouldn't be bothered until he felt more human.

About nine fifteen, there was a peremptory knock at the door and Bob Fellows bustled in. His face was flushed and excited. 'We've had a call from PC Hargreaves. Apparently, he's on the track of the killer – or so he believes. He's following by car. He's in one of the mufti models. He'll need back-up.'

Snow was out of his chair in an instant. 'Let's go,' he barked, almost cheerful that there was some action at last to divert his mind.

'The latest is that he's through the centre of town and heading up towards Outlane. He's driving a grey Ford

Escort van, registration number CHD 825V. Hargreaves thinks that he's got the girl in the back of the van.' Bob Fellows conveyed this information in staccato fashion as he drove the car at great speed out of the HQ car park and on to the main road.

Snow nodded sternly. He was unsure in his own mind whether he wanted this young copper to be right or wrong. If the girl was in the van, the chances are that she was already dead.

'For the moment, we must leave the matter in Hargreaves' hands while we follow this up. We don't want any patrol car getting in on the act. If he sees a police vehicle on his tail, who knows what crazy thing he'll do.'

'Yes, sir,' said Fellows, happy to let his boss make decisions in this volatile situation.

Snatching up the intercom, Snow made contact with Hargreaves.

'DI Snow here. We're coming after you. Please detail your current location.'

'Hello, sir,' came the crackly response. Even through the tiny speaker Snow could gauge the tension in his policeman's voice. 'I'm just two cars behind the suspect, travelling up New Hey Road. He's taking it fairly steady and luckily for me the traffic is still rather heavy from the morning rush. We're about two minutes from Outlane village.'

'Good man. Make sure you hold him in sight and keep us in touch with his movements. We must not lose him at any cost.'

'Yes, sir.'

Snow switched off the intercom. 'Outlane,' he muttered. 'Looks like he might be headed out on to the moors.'

'To dispose of the body.'

Snow narrowed his eyes, and stared resolutely at the road ahead without replying.

Hirst passed through the small village of Outlane, and soon undulating fields were flowing past on either side of him. The road ribboned off in a fairly straight fashion up towards the moors and the Lancashire border. Those moors. That bleak terrain forever associated with Myra Hindley and Ian Brady, the murderers who had buried their young victims up there in unmarked graves. No doubt he would be compared to them. Evil child killers. But he was not like them. They were mad murderers who killed for kicks, for pure pleasure. There was no purpose, no reason behind their killings. He wasn't mad and he wasn't evil. He had a real motive for doing what he was doing. He was an angel of justice, balancing those scales that God had tipped the wrong way. He derived no enjoyment from his actions, a dark satisfaction perhaps, because he was performing a duty to his wife and his lovely daughter. He was righting a major wrong. When all this was over, he would join them. If at all possible, he would not wait to be captured. Once he had completed his task, he would have nothing to live for. His death would be the fitting final chapter in this bleak story.

As the road rose towards the dim horizon, as though waiting to be enfolded by the barren moors, the sky seemed to grow darker and the clouds loured above the bleak countryside as though waiting in misty ambush. But Hirst was not headed for the moors. He had another destination in mind.

'He's turned left off the main road, sir. I think he's making for Scammonden Dam reservoir.'

'Are there any other vehicles on the road with you apart from Hirst's van?' asked Snow.

'No, sir.'

'Well, for God's sake keep him in view but stay well back. He must not twig that you're following him.'

'I understand, sir.'

'We're not far behind you now. Just watch and wait.'

'Will do, sir.'

Hirst manoeuvred the van at moderate speed along the narrow twisting roads which led towards the great man-made stretch of water that was the Scammonden Dam. His mind was so concentrated on his driving and the act he intended to commit when he reached his destination, the visitor's car park which was perched high above the dam, that he failed to spot the black Corsa some two hundred yards behind him.

Hirst pulled into the car park area. There was just one other vehicle parked at the far end. There was no sign of the driver. Hirst assumed that he was a walker and was somewhere along the water's edge, making a circular tour of the dam. He knew this was a popular pursuit for casual walkers.

He got out of the van and walked all the way around it, checking there was no one else in the vicinity. When he was convinced he was alone in this windswept spot, he opened the back doors, clambered inside and pulled them to again. The sports bag lay there in the shadows. Carefully he pulled down the zip and folded back the sides of the bag to expose the body within.

The girl moved slightly, the rush of cool air assailing her senses. As he knelt down beside her, she opened her eyes.

They were glazed and sleepy and not really seeing clearly. All she could make out was a dark shape gently shifting by her side.

Her lips parted slightly and she spoke, her voice emerging like an elongated purr.

'Daddy,' she said. And then repeated it. 'Daddy.'

The word shocked and horrified Hirst. His body grew rigid and his heart throbbed with anguish. She had thought that he was … he was … My God, and she sounded just like …

Suddenly with an acid ice-cold ferocity, the veils were lifted from his twisted, corrupted mind. It came like a lightning bolt to his brain, waking, shaking him from his mad dream. That little girl's voice calling for her daddy. His body vibrated with shock and emotion. It was as though he was suddenly fully aware of what he had done and what he was about to do, with a searing, heart-wrenching clarity. This little, sleepy creature before him was the same age as his daughter, could be his daughter, with all her future ahead of her and he was about to kill her. To take her life. And what for?

He clutched his chest in agony as the realisation of this horror coursed through his body. He sank to his knees, emitting a strangled moan.

The girl shifted again, the eyelids fluttering and her little tongue emerging to moisten her lips.

And that word came once more like a dagger in his breast: 'Daddy.'

For a moment time seemed to stand still. The world stopped and silence thudded in his ears. But that word, uttered by the soft, drowsy voice, lingered in the air, burrowing like some malignant worm in his ear: 'Daddy.'

He opened his mouth to speak, to utter something, he knew not what, but no sound came. He had no idea what to do now. He couldn't kill the girl. Not now. How could he? Not now that he had seen, had realised how wrong, how futile, how evil he had been. How could he take this girl away from her … her daddy? He ran his hand over his face, the fingers pinching his features, hard enough to cause him pain. If only this could be some horrible dream.

And then the world returned; the silence faded and he heard a noise behind him. The doors of the van swung open with a violent clang, light flooded in and a dark figure sprang forward. Before he could react in any way, Hirst felt an arm around his neck and a gruff voice muttered close to his ear, 'Got you, you bastard.'

For a brief moment, his body relaxed as he quickly took in the situation and accepted it. He didn't know how this had happened but he knew he was being apprehended. Remarkably, for a moment this brought him a frisson of relief. He no longer had to make decisions about the girl. He could now succumb to the whims of fate. But as the hold on his neck grew tighter, the sense of self-preservation overwhelmed these insubstantial, fleeting feelings. The innate instinct for survival rose within him, and with a ferocity he did not know he possessed, he rose up and with a roar he thrust his body backwards, ramming his assailant against the wall of the van.

With a cry of pain, PC Hargreaves slumped to the floor. He was dazed and winded but still conscious. But not for long.

Hirst, now acting on a basic animal instinct, lashed out with his fists, beating hard against Hargreaves' face, sending the policeman's head ricocheting backwards, crashing against the metal wall, rendering him unconscious immediately.

With a simian growl, Hirst leapt out of the back of the van and raced towards the path that led down towards the dam.

TWENTY

He entered the house with ease. Breaking and entering gently was one of the tricks of his trade. He was tempted to give the place a thorough search, but that was not the purpose of his visit and besides he knew that the occupant was a careful enough fellow not to leave anything that might incriminate him within easy reach. If there was anything at all – and that was doubtful, knowing this man – it would be hidden where no one could find it.

But, as he had already asserted to himself, this was not why he was making this particular house call. He wanted to spook the bastard. This was only the beginning. He smiled at the prospect. That smile was the only thing about his demeanour that gave any hint to his growing mental instability.

Now, should he put the two together or … separately? He decided on separately. In placing the items in different rooms he would provide two surprises or, preferably, two shocks. Shocks would be better. His aim was to produce gasps and cold sweats, not merely raised eyebrows. He giggled at this notion and then performed his tasks with speed.

Within minutes, he had closed the door and was walking towards his car, a very large self-satisfied grin plastered on his face.

TWENTY-ONE

Snow and Fellows were just pulling into the little car park overlooking Scammonden Dam when they saw Frank Hirst leap out of the grey Ford van and head off into the undergrowth.

'You see to the girl – if she's in there. I'll get after Hirst,' snapped Snow, quickly assessing the situation. He jumped out the car and hared off in the direction Hirst had taken.

As he reached the pathway which snaked its way through the trees down to the water's edge, Snow spotted Hirst about a hundred yards ahead of him, making speedy progress. Summoning an extra burst of speed, Snow followed. It was eerily quiet around the dam. There was no rustle of wind in the trees or the sound of birds, just the faint swish of two pairs of feet racing through the dry grass.

'Stop, police!' cried Snow loudly, breaking that silence, knowing that this was a futile exclamation, but he felt obliged to use it. At least he was warning the bastard that the authorities were on his tail.

His voice trailed over the dead air and for a brief moment his cry caused Hirst to pause and turn round. On seeing Snow, he resumed his flight.

Within minutes both men had reached the pathway that circumnavigated the giant dam, but the chase continued. Snow was gaining ground but then suddenly Hirst left the path and made his way out on to a promontory which stuck out like a rocky finger into the choppy waters. Reaching the end of it, without a moment's hesitation, Hirst flung himself into the water.

'What the hell?' muttered Snow in disbelief. 'What is the man up to?' The answer came to him immediately. 'He's bloody well going to try and drown himself. Well, he bloody well isn't. That's too easy a way out for him.'

With gritted teeth Snow followed suit. He dashed along the rocks and plunged into the murky water. He gave an involuntary gasp as his body reacted to the shock of the fierce cold that enveloped his body. It was as though all the oxygen was being forcibly pumped from his lungs. He gulped for air while desperately scanning the surface for any signs of Hirst. He spotted him about fifteen yards to his left. With grim determination he struck out towards his quarry, but as he drew nearer, he saw the man disappear beneath the chill grey waters. This confirmed to Snow that he was indeed intending to drown himself. That's if he didn't die of hypothermia first.

Snow was a fair swimmer and soon reached the spot where Hirst had vanished, realising that now he would have to dive down beneath the rippling surface after him. He knew that he couldn't think too much about this procedure or else he would lose the impetus, the courage to do it. Already his body was shaking with cold and his limbs felt stiff and unresponsive. Taking a deep breath, he sank down under the waves. It was far gloomier than he expected: a wall of shifting grey water met his eyes, thick as a pea-souper fog and just as impenetrable. He swam a few feet, peering desperately into the darkness without success, and then surfaced once more, gasping and gulping, partially to fill his lungs with air and partially as a reaction to the Arctic cold that was slowly conquering his body. As he broke the surface, so did Frank Hirst, some ten feet away. The man was also spluttering and coughing, his arms flailing wildly in a frantic fashion. It was obvious to Snow that this heartless killer was finding it far more difficult to do away with himself than he had to take the lives of young girls.

As he began to swim towards this thrashing shape in the water, a dark thought entered his mind. Wouldn't it be a lot simpler for all concerned if he just drowned the bugger himself? Held his head under the water while reciting the names of the young victims whose lives he had taken, while his squirming body twisted and turned in the icy depths. Hold him down until the struggles grew less and the bloated body grew limp. That would be simpler and less costly to a society that would have to cough up the funds for the trial and the long prison sentence Hirst would eventually receive. His hurt to society would not be over with his capture.

As he grabbed Hirst by the shoulders, it was very tempting just to thrust him downwards until his head dipped beneath the water and keep it there. But it was a temptation that Snow could resist. He was not that kind of man. Although he didn't believe in God, he was not about to assume the role himself. His job, his duty, was to bring this man in and see that he was charged for the crimes he had committed. That's where his responsibility ended, morally and professionally. To do more would be wrong.

At first Hirst struggled to pull himself free as Snow began to tug him towards the shore, but very quickly he gave in to the inevitable. He was exhausted physically and mentally. The fight had gone out of him and he simply surrendered to events.

Eventually, with much effort, Snow was able to haul his weighty charge up on to the rocky shore. By now Hirst was only just conscious. He had swallowed great amounts of water and the dramatic events of the last ten minutes had gradually caused his brain to shut down.

Snow was also cold and exhausted but his steely nature prevented him from succumbing to the overwhelming sense of fatigue that he felt. He had a job to do. He slapped Hirst around the face to rouse him. He was damned if he was going to carry this bastard back up to the car park.

When the eyes flickered open and focused vaguely on him, the policeman announced in a hoarse voice that he was arresting him for murder. Like an automaton, he recited the standard rhetoric, before dragging Hirst to his feet and hauling him along the shoreline towards the pathway which led to the car park at the top.

Meanwhile, Bob Fellows had been ministering to the girl. He had retrieved a fruit drink from the glove compartment of his car and allowed her to sip from it gently. She was very groggy but apart from that she appeared to be unharmed. After a few sips, she relaxed again and slipped back into sleep. Then Fellows turned his attention to PC Hargreaves who still lay sprawled on the floor of the van. Bob quickly ascertained that he had not been shot and was just concussed. There was a nasty bump on the back of his head and a small cut on the scalp. The big lad would live.

Satisfied that both his patients were safe for the time being without his presence, Bob ventured to the edge of the car park, wondering what had happened to his boss and if he needed his help. Peering down towards the dam, he glimpsed Snow through the trees, dragging Frank Hirst up the pathway. They resembled two drowned rats. Fellows made his way down towards them.

'Are you OK, sir?'

'I will be when I can dry off. Get the cuffs on this fellow. I've read him his rights. How is the girl?'

'She's alive. She's just been drugged. Chloroform, I think. But she'll be OK.'

'Thank heavens.'

'I've rung for an ambulance,' Fellows added as he clamped the handcuffs over Hirst's wrists. He did not react in any way, his head lolling on his chest, eyes staring at the ground.

'Let's get him to headquarters. I'll be a lot happier when he's stowed away in a cell,' said Snow.

'Sure thing, sir. Well done. What a relief it's all over, eh?'

Snow, very damp and exhausted, gave a brief nod. For some reason he did not feel any relief or sense of closure.

TWENTY-TWO

Two hours later, Snow was sitting in his office with his third cup of coffee, hunched up in his chair, still feeling the chill of the icy waters. He'd borrowed an old police sergeant's uniform while his suit and shirt had been taken out to be dry cleaned.

Elizabeth Saunders' parents had been informed of the situation and they were with their daughter at the hospital. Apparently, apart from some drowsiness still remaining as the after-effect of the chloroform, she was fine and would be well enough to go home within a few hours. She was a tough little girl and did not seem too alarmed by her ordeal. PC Hargreaves had also recovered consciousness but was still suffering from concussion and was being kept in overnight for observation.

'I really think you should go home, sir. Have a hot toddy and get to bed. You've had a serious soaking. You don't want to catch your death of cold, do you?'

Snow laughed at his sergeant. 'I've never noticed these mother hen tendencies in you before, Bob,' he said. 'Perhaps you'd like to come home with me and tuck me up.'

'I think I'll draw the line there.'

'I'm fine. Still a bit damp behind the ears but I'll feel a lot better once I'm back in my own my suit. I feel like a pantomime Mr Plod in this baggy outfit. However, I must admit I don't feel up to filling in the paperwork just now.'

'I'm not surprised. The interview with Hirst and his solicitor is in the morning, is that right?'

Snow nodded. 'Yeah. He had no objection to waiting. In fact, he has been docile and virtually mute since I dragged him out of the water.'

'Bastard.'

Snow twisted his features. 'I reckon there's more to it than that.'

'If you don't mind me saying so, sir, sometimes you look for deeper meanings when there aren't any. This is a simple case of loony killer goes on the rampage and then gets caught.'

'Simple case?'

'Yes, sir.'

'Whatever,' he said diplomatically. It was you, Bob, he thought, who often didn't look deep enough into matters. Nothing is ever as simple as it appears on the surface. 'However,' he added, 'I am ducking out of the formalities at this juncture. I've handed over proceedings to DI Osborne. He'll be with you in the interview room tomorrow.'

'What! You're passing this over now.'

'Yes. I've had my fill of it and I'm sure it will be straightforward anyway. The fellow's confessed. There will be no conflict.'

Before Bob Fellows could respond, there was a brief knock at the door and Susan Morgan bustled in, holding a suit carrier so that it didn't drag along the ground.

'Hello, sir. Your suit, shirt and tie, dry, pressed and ready to wear.'

Snow beamed. 'You are an angel,' he said and then blushed slightly when he realised what he'd said.

'I have friends at Easy Clean and when I said these were the clothes of the detective who had hauled in the child-killer, they did the business quick sticks and for nothing.'

'You see, sir, there are some perks to being a copper.' observed Bob Fellows.

'So it seems. Thanks, Susan. Much appreciated.' Snow took the suit carrier from her with a smile. 'Now if you two don't mind, I'd like the privacy to change out of this smelly old uniform back into my own clothes.'

'What you need is a phone box to change from mild-mannered copper to Super Snow,' grinned Bob, ushering Susan out of the office with a smile.

Ten minutes later, back in his own clothes and feeling very much his old self, DI Paul Snow emerged from his office and was greeted by a mild ripple of applause from the small group of officers there. He was, it seemed, the hero of the hour for bringing in Frank Hirst. No doubt Bob Fellows had overdramatised the event, as was his wont, but this reaction amused and pleased Snow. He accepted the approbation with a gentle smile and a wave of the hand as he moved swiftly through the room into the cool corridor beyond. His smile faded as he made his way down into the basement where the cells were located.

PC Braithwaite was gatekeeper and he seemed surprised to see Snow.

'I've come to see Hirst,' he said quietly. He knew this was not protocol. He should have another officer and Hirst's solicitor with him for this to happen.

Braithwaite hesitated. He didn't want to challenge a senior officer but he knew the rules.

'I won't be long. Nothing serious. It'll just help the case. You understand,' said Snow gently, placing a friendly hand on Braithwaite's shoulders.

The constable, like most of the officers at the station, respected and even admired Snow for his diligence and professionalism and his considered treatment of the lower ranks. He was all right was old Snow, was the mantra in the canteen. It was because of this general feeling that Braithwaite acceded to Snow's request.

'Don't be too long, sir,' he added sotto voce as he led Snow down a narrow corridor to Hirst's cell.

'No, I won't,' came the murmured reply.

Frank Hirst sat hunched up on the small pallet bed in the cell, a blanket around his shoulders. His hands were clenched and he was staring at the far wall in front of him. He was now dressed in standard issue prison wear but his hair was still damp and flattened to his scalp. He looked like a bedraggled statue and did not move one inch as Snow entered the cell.

The policeman pulled up a chair and sat close to him and waited a few seconds to see if the man would react. He did not.

'I just want to know, why?' said Snow quietly. 'Tell me why, Frank. Explain it to me.'

Hirst's face remained immobile.

'There must be so much you want to get off your chest. Now's your chance. Now's your chance before you are hounded by police officers, lawyers and others. Those that will twist your words and motive.'

Still not a flicker on the prisoner's face.

'This is unofficial. Nothing is being recorded. I just want to know why ... why you killed those girls.'

Slowly Hirst raised his head and turned his watery eyes towards Snow. His lips trembled momentarily before he spoke. 'Daddy.' The word emerged as a tortured whisper. 'She said, "Daddy".'

'Who said that?'

'The girl. Elizabeth. She said "Daddy". She thought … she thought that I …'

Tears trickled down Hirst's face and it froze in an agonised stare.

Snow wasn't quite sure what Hirst was talking about but he knew instinctively that he should remain silent and wait. He had begun talking now and the policeman felt fairly certain that the dam would break soon and the information he was seeking would cascade out.

Hirst wiped the tears away with his sleeve. 'Have you got kids?' he asked.

Snow shook his head.

'You can't understand then.'

'Try me. As a police officer I've seen a lot and understand a lot. You get to dig deep into feelings. Outsiders often see more.'

Hirst thought about this for a moment and then said: 'I had a daughter. Debbie. Little Debbie. She was the light of my life. Little … She meant the world to me. No doubt, people thought I doted on her too much. Worshipped her. We both did, me and my wife.'

Snow nodded judiciously.

'Don't get me wrong: I loved my wife, too, and she loved me, but we channelled our …' He struggled to find the right word. 'We channelled our passion into her. Our lives were dull, mundane, humdrum but hers … was like a rainbow. Full of colours and excitement.' For a fleeting moment his face twisted into a crooked smile which even reached his eyes.

'And then,' he continued, his voice growing stronger now and his body posture more relaxed, 'she was taken away from us. Cruelly. Without warning. Killed. Without reason. One minute she was kissing me goodbye and hugging me tight and the next she was torn and blood-ied on a slab like a piece of meat in the butchers.'

'That must have been terrible.' Snow meant it. He had the imagination and sensitivity to empathise completely.

'Terrible doesn't touch the half of it. Why her? Why was my beautiful daughter crushed in that coach? Why was she one of those who died? It's a question I asked a thousand times. It bore like a drill in my head. Why couldn't she have lived?'

There was no answer to that one and Snow was not about to attempt to provide one.

'It was so unfair. I mean ... if she deserved to die, the others did as well. That's only fair.'

'But she wasn't the only one to be killed in the crash. There were others who died,' Snow suggested gently.

Hirst shook his head in agreement. 'I know, I know. But what bit into my soul, kept me awake at nights, was the thought of those who by a whim of chance had got away with it. They'd missed out on death.'

'You saw it as their fault that they had survived?'

'Yes. They were the smug ones walking away from the twisted wreck unharmed, able to carry on living while Debbie was placed in a coffin. What did they care as they returned home to their lovely, little happy lives? They were all right. They could laugh again. Laugh without a thought for my poor darling, their dead friend. They forgot her. It didn't matter to them because they were all right. It wasn't fair. Don't you understand?

It wasn't bloody fair! That's what haunted me. That's what ate away at my brain. That's what drove me on.'

Hirst gulped for air and clutched his hands together in a wringing motion as his emotions overtook him again.

Snow waited.

'And then my Pam went,' he resumed after a moment. 'She felt the same pain as me but in a different way. While mine smouldered like a bonfire, growing hotter and angrier, she gave in to despair. The door on her future had been slammed in her face when our Debbie died. I was no use to her. Debbie had been our link and now that had gone. There was nothing to hold us together. Living … just living became too much for her. Making a cup of tea, having a sandwich, reading a book – which she used to love – meant nothing to her any more. So … she took her life. Jumped off a bridge on to the bloody motorway. Splat!' He gave an agonised cry halfway between a wail and a laugh, both horrified and amused at his expression. 'I had no idea that she'd do it. To be honest I didn't think she had it in her. I mean it takes some guts to jump off a bridge … but I can say that if I'd known what she intended to do, I wouldn't have stopped her. It was the only way that she could have prevented her suffering. Living was now just pain and only death was the escape.'

'But you didn't think like this.'

Hirst shook his head vigorously. 'No. I wanted revenge and when Pam went, the flames of that bonfire I mentioned consumed me. Her death spurred me on.'

'To do what?'

Hirst's face twisted again into that dark, mad smile. 'You know what. It was mad, wasn't it? *I* was mad, wasn't I?

I thought that by killing those girls, those blessed survivors, I would somehow be justifying Debbie's death, her cruel and unfair death. If she had to die, they should, too.'

With a brisk, angry motion, he ran his fingers through his hair.

'It gave me a purpose, you see,' he continued, his whole demeanour becoming more animated now. 'I had a reason to get up in the morning. That's what I was living for. I planned each one – each killing – meticulously. It was imperative that I wasn't caught before I had completed all five. I was in some kind of demented trance. Reality and logic had drifted away from me. I see that now. I see that now. I was a monster. A deranged animal. I know it's no excuse to say grief made me that way. It's true but it's not a fucking excuse, is it?'

'No,' Snow said softly.

'And do you know what lifted the veil, what suddenly made me see what I had done? What I had become.'

'Tell me.'

'It was that little girl, Elizabeth. In the van. Up at Scammonden. There I was leaning over her, ready to strangle her to death and … God help me … she opened her eyes and called me "Daddy". She thought that dark monster looming over her … "Daddy" she said, in that same soft sleepy voice that Debbie used to use. Then it hit me like a fucking ten-ton truck. My head exploded. I saw clearly what I had done. How wrong I had been.'

Suddenly Hirst's body stiffened and his arms reached out for Snow without actually touching him. The detective remained calm and still.

'Hey, don't get me wrong. I'm not asking for sympathy or anything like that. I deserve all that's coming to me. Whether you're recording this or not, I don't care. I am guilty. Guilty as hell and hell is where I belong. I killed those girls. Those poor innocent girls. That's what you wanted to hear, wasn't it?'

Not really, thought, Snow. I knew that. There can be no doubt that you are guilty and will serve a life sentence. What I really wanted to know is what drove you to do such terrible acts and now I do. But Snow kept these thoughts to himself. Instead he replied: 'As I said, I'm not recording this interview. This is a private visit, but I sincerely recommend you inform the interviewing officers tomorrow all you have told me.'

'Sure. Why not? It won't do me any good and why should it? I don't want it to. I don't deserve sympathy or mercy. I just want to die now. I deserve to die. Not to be locked away for years. I'll still be eating, sleeping and functioning after a fashion when I should be rotting in some grave somewhere.'

Snow had no answer for this. He knew the death penalty was not only barbaric but also made no allowance for any miscarriage of justice, but in cases like Hirst's when the perpetrator is drowned in remorse, perhaps the rope would be the best solution for all concerned. He was sure the mothers of the three murdered girls would support that notion.

'Thank you,' said Snow, rising from his chair.

'What for?'

'For being honest with me. I cannot feel sympathy for you. The faces of those dead girls would haunt my dreams forever if I did that, but I now understand why you did what you did and as a police officer that is important to know. And, as I say, I thank you for that.'

'What did the bastard have to say for himself?' snarled PC Braithwaite as he locked up the cell again.

'Not much,' said Snow.

'Nah, these looneys always keep it stashed up here.' He tapped the side of his head. 'Don't think they know themselves why they do what they do.'

Snow nodded noncommittally.

A headache was building steadily and with some ferocity around Snow's temple as he returned to his office. Suddenly he felt very weary and strangely depressed. Time he went home, he thought, take some paracetemol and get an early night. He was just reaching for his coat when Bob Fellows popped his head round the door.

'Thought you might fancy a pint, sir, as a kind of celebration. Catching the bugger, like.'

Snow was about to shake his head and refuse when he had a sudden change of mind. A fuggy pub and a few pints in cheery company might be exactly what he needed. It was likely to be more effective than pills and that early night for easing his spirits.

'Why not,' he said, managing to raise a smile.

It was now around five o'clock and although the County was reasonably quiet, it was starting to fill up with workers catching a quick drink on their way home. The warm, blurry atmosphere wrapped itself around the two policemen as they entered, protecting them from the harsh realities of soberland outside. Snow and Fellows secured a quiet corner seat in the back snug. Bob raised his glass and clinked it against Snow's.

'Cheers.'

Snow gave a smile that he did not feel. 'It seems wrong in a way, celebrating like this. There are three dead girls that we failed to save.'

Bob gave an exaggerated grimace. 'I know. But we did our best. The odds were really stacked against us. And had we not eventually been successful, there would have been more killings.'

Two more, to be precise, thought Snow. He saw the logic of Bob's observation but it did not alter the strange sense of sadness he felt at the girls' deaths, a mixture of guilt and despair. He knew that it would pass in time and, ironically, this fact added to his unhappiness. We soon forget the pain and the treachery as the wheel of life spins on.

'Come on, drink up, sir. My round next,' said Bob cheerfully, before draining a good third of his pint.

Attempting to shrug off his bleak thoughts, Snow mimicked his sergeant, taking a large gulp of the cold, harsh brew. He hoped that it would help soften the hard edges of his dark mood.

Two pints later those dark edges were well and truly softened as were, to some extent, Snow's brain and tongue. While not exactly drunk, he knew that he was not fully in control of his body or his speech. If anything, Bob Fellows was far worse and was about to switch drinks and go on to the whisky. Time, thought Snow sluggishly, to move, to get moving, to leave, to absent himself, to hightail to the hills. To go home. He grinned inanely to himself as his mind ran along this particular tautological gamut. He was sober enough to realise he was not fit to drive and that he'd have to leave his car behind at HQ and take a taxi home.

He rose a little unsteadily, desperate to keep his uncertain limbs in check. It wouldn't do for a DI to be seen stumbling out of a pub in a tipsy fashion. 'I'm making tracks, Bob,' he said, adding another interpretation to his actions and aware that his diction was not as clear as he would have liked.

'One for the road, sir, eh?' Bob waggled his glass temptingly.

Snow shook his head. 'I'm fine,' he said, feeling far from it.

The cool night air came as a shock to him, making his head seem even lighter. Why, he pondered, is it with alcohol that one always goes one drink too many? Two pints would have been sufficient. He had felt better after two, but the third had allowed the depressive thoughts to return. With a slow, steady gait he made his way along town to St George's Square by the station and secured a taxi to take him home.

Once there, he felt the indignity of the situation as he fumbled with his key, which failed several times to slip into the aperture and allow him to turn it. Eventually, he gained access and, slamming the door behind him, he slumped to the floor thoroughly exhausted. He remained in this position for ten minutes or so, dozing a little, no longer fighting the alcohol in his system.

Coffee, he thought after a while. That's what I need. With the movement of an infirm geriatric, he struggled to his feet and made his way into the kitchen. He filled the kettle and secured the mug and jar of coffee before he saw it. It was on the work surface near the hob: a bottle of champagne. It had a bright pink ribbon tied around the neck and a card dangling from the side. Snow frowned. His alcohol-dulled brain could not make this one out. What was the bottle doing there? How had it got there? He hadn't put it there. So, someone else had. That meant that someone had been in his house. With the laborious working out of this, his mind sharpened as the disturbing reality took hold.

He tore off the card and read the message inscribed on it: 'To Pauley, all my love, CB xxx'.

It did not take Snow long to work out the meaning of the message and more significantly the implications.

'The bastard's been in my house. Colin Bird,' he grunted, throwing the card down. He glanced around him desperately, as though he was expecting Bird to pop up by the sink unit. He rushed into the sitting room and froze in the doorway, for there on the little coffee table was an enormous bunch of flowers in a glass vase. Again there was a card loosely attached to the side. This time it read: 'Here's hoping our love blooms like these pretty flowers. All my love, Pauley – from CB.'

Instinctively and irrationally, emitting a growl of fury, Paul knocked the vase over with a swipe of his hand, water spraying on the carpet and the glass vase cracking as it hit the floor, spilling the blooms at his feet. What on earth was the mad devil playing at? Was he really this delusional, thinking there was a future in a relationship together, or was this some kind of crazy scheme to unnerve him, the man who had rejected his advances? And how the hell had he got into his house? Well, on quick reflection there was no mystery in that. He was a policeman. He would have ways.

Snow slumped down on the sofa and ran his fingers through his hair. Suddenly he felt very sober. Yes, he had a thumping headache, but the mists of inebriation had cleared. In this shiny new clarity, the question raised itself like a leviathan from the deep: what the hell was he going to do about Colin Bird?

TWENTY-THREE

PC Arnold Braithwaite was on duty again the following morning, relieving his colleague PC Newman, who had been down in the cells overnight. 'Lucky me,' Braithwaite growled, 'just in time to deliver the bastard's breakfast. I hope it chokes him.'

Newman nodded. 'Save us all a lot of bother and the taxpayer a wallop of dosh if it did.'

Braithwaite gazed down at the tray holding the plate with a piece of greasy bacon, a pallid fried egg and a small congealed mound of anaemic baked beans. 'I'd love to slip a little arsenic into this lot.' He chuckled at the thought and then made his way down to the narrow corridor to Frank Hirst's cell.

While holding the tray in one hand, he slid aside the metal spyhole cover. The sight that met his eyes caused him to drop the tray, the sound of which resounded noisily down the corridor. In the grey light of the cell afforded by the barred window and the feeble light bulb, PC Braithwaite could just make out two legs dangling by the wall. He really didn't need to see any more to know what had happened.

'Like death warmed up.' Snow had heard the expression bandied about the station before when some of the younger officers had come in the morning following a night on the lash. Now he knew what it meant, for this morning he was experiencing a very similar feeling. He felt like death warmed up. It was partly the after-effects of the booze imbibed in the County and partly his concerns about Colin Bird, and in particular what to do about this maverick crazy man. He had no idea what kind of stupid stunt he would try to pull next.

As soon as Snow reached HQ, he made himself another strong coffee, the fourth that morning, and hid himself away in his office. Some thirty minutes later, Bob Fellows knocked and entered. If Snow had thought he looked a little rough that morning in the shaving mirror, it was nothing to the ghoul-like figure that hovered before him now. He walked gingerly as though passing with naked feet over burning coals, and his eyes, dark rimmed, had almost sunken into his face, the skin of which had the texture of tissue paper.

'Good morning, sir,' he croaked.

Snow could not help but smile. 'Feeling a little delicate, are we Sergeant?'

Fellows nodded and it was clear that he found the action of moving his head quite painful.

The conversation, such as it was, got no further for Susan Morgan opened the door. Her expression was severe. 'Hirst has topped himself,' she said sharply and succinctly.

'What?' Snow rose from his chair.

'He made a rope-type noose out of his shirt and vest and hung himself in his cell. He was found at breakfast time this morning.'

'Bloody hell,' said Fellows.

Snow sat down again as the reality of the situation sank in. He swallowed the words that were on the tip of his tongue because he considered perhaps that they were inappropriate. He was about to say, 'Perhaps it was for the best', but thought better of it. Instead, he said, 'Looks like he couldn't live with the guilt. Well, in effect that draws a very firm line under this very unpleasant case.'

'Too true. Typical, he took the coward's way out,' observed Fellows, his pallid features regaining some of their colour as he grew more animated. 'I bet those parents who lost their kids will be delighted. Let's face it, prison is a soft option for bastards like Hirst who kill young 'uns for no reason. He deserved to die.'

'That's one way of looking at it,' said Susan coolly, 'but he cheated the system at the last.'

'So what, the bugger's dead. Good riddance.'

Snow glanced at Susan, their eyes connecting. It was clear to each of them what both were thinking: how wonderful to have such an uncomplicated black and white view of things like Bob Fellows. It would make life so much simpler.

TWENTY-FOUR

If it was the simple life that Snow craved, then the gods in charge of his destiny appeared to grant him his wish, for a week or so at least. After the furore of Frank Hirst's death had died down and the papers, after blaming the police for their incompetence in allowing a major criminal to kill himself while in their care, had found other scapegoats to pillory, things went quiet for Snow at police HQ. It was just paperwork and a few unremarkable enquiries to follow up. He welcomed the respite from the stress of the Hirst case. Of course, there was the little demon of the Colin Bird situation still sitting on his shoulder, but there had been no further developments in that department either. He was thankful for the relief.

Snow had done a little gentle digging and discovered that Bird had taken himself off on a protracted leave, possibly, he pondered, so that he could lick his wounds. Snow felt a shaft of guilt about this. He was not conscious of giving off any signs that he was interested in Bird or prepared to start a relationship with him, but something must have created this impression in the man's mind and maybe this was something he had done or said. What still worried Snow was the fact that Bird was an irrational and unpredictable character and there was always the possibility that he could create further mischief.

One of his more pleasant duties in the days following Frank Hirst's death was welcoming PC Hargreaves back to his duties after his brief stay in hospital. The young constable was fully recovered from his minor injuries and was thrilled that Snow had added a commendation to his record for his contribution to the apprehension and arrest of Hirst. There were still some rough edges to Hargreaves, thought Snow, but he had the right attitude and intelligence which should take him far. He reckoned that in all probability he'd have his sergeant's stripes within a few years.

Elizabeth Saunders had also left hospital and Snow and Fellows had paid a courtesy call at home. Snow was pleased to see that physically the girl seemed fine, although she seemed ill at ease with them, strangers in her own home. The medics had said it would take some time before she was able to relax with men she didn't know. Strangers made her very uneasy. Not surprisingly, thought Snow. Nevertheless, the girl was determined to return to school as soon as possible, which showed a remarkable spirit.

So all seemed reasonably quiet once more on Snow's pond.

And then all hell broke loose.

Snow was settling down for an evening in front of the television when he got the call. He wasn't much of a viewer but once in a while he enjoyed relaxing as the homogenised pap that the TV companies churned out washed over him. It took him out of himself and helped wash the mental grime of the day away. The shrill call of the phone, like a distant scream, put an end to his viewing plans. He switched the set off even before he answered the phone.

'Bad news, sir,' said Bob Fellows at the other end.

'Yes.'

'Elizabeth Saunders has gone missing. She never made it home from school.'

'What?' Initially Snow had difficulty comprehending what his sergeant was saying.

'I'm afraid it looks like she may have been kidnapped.'

Snow shook his head in disbelief. This was crazy. Unreal. He took a few seconds before responding to get himself thinking straight. 'Is there any evidence to support that? Couldn't she just have gone off somewhere? Be at a friend's house.' He knew these were probably pointless assertions. Bob would not have made the statement about kidnapping without good reason.

'There is evidence.' Fellows paused as though he was too embarrassed to continue. 'The parents received a telephone call about twenty minutes ago. From the kidnapper.'

'Asking for a ransom?'

'No, sir. He just said. "I've got Lizzie. I'm finishing the job off. Tell Inspector Snow, catch me if you can".'

Snow's stomach constricted violently and he found himself clasping the receiver with a fierce grip in his sweaty hand. 'Finishing the job off,' he repeated slowly.

'Yes, sir. It looks like whoever this joker is, he's taken up the baton dropped by Hirst.'

Again Snow took time to think before replying. It was difficult not to believe that he was dreaming. The hissing silence unnerved Fellows.

'Are you still there, sir?'

'Yes, yes, I'm just trying to get my head round this. I'm fairly certain that Hirst was working alone. This is not the action of a partner in crime.'

'It could be someone who was sympathetic to Hirst's cause. Someone else who lost their child in that crash.'

Snow thought that very unlikely, but his ragged brain could not offer up any sensible suggestion at the moment so he turned his thoughts to more practical matters. 'When was the girl last seen?'

'At school. I don't know the details. These need to be checked.'

'Is someone with the parents now?'

'Yes.'

'They need twenty-four-hour surveillance and we need to have the phone tapped in case the abductor rings again.'

'I'll get on to it.'

'Good man. Alert patrol cars and bobbies on the beat with the girl's description. I'll see you early in the office. At seven. We need to go to the school and find out exactly when the girl was last seen and take our investigation from there.'

'Right, sir.'

Snow replaced the receiver and gazed at his reflection in the hall mirror. He could see the sheen of sweat on his forehead and the look of desperation in his eyes. Within minutes the relaxed fellow who had planned a night in front of the telly had become a haunted man. What the hell was going on? Why had this girl been taken? And why, for God's sake, had his name been mentioned? It seemed that this time the whole thing was personal.

TWENTY-FIVE

He looked down on the sleeping girl with mixed emotions. He was a little frightened that his resolution was wavering. Could he really kill this pretty little thing? Had he gone one step too far in his plans? He bit his lip deliberately to cause himself some pain, to bring him back from this wavering realm. He had to stop thinking about this. He had designed and made his elaborate bed and now he must lie on it.

Was he mad? he wondered as he locked the room. If he was, he didn't feel it. Angry? Yes. Determined? He was getting there. Excited? Certainly. He had to admit to himself that the emotions that rippled through his consciousness now were for the main part exhilarating. They stimulated and invigorated him. They released him from the straitjacket of conformity, duty and mundanity. He was getting his own back by upsetting someone who had very seriously upset him, but who had also given him the freedom to leap over the fence and break rules. Very serious rules. He smiled at this concept. Yes, yes, of course he was doing the right thing. He would go downstairs and have a drink to celebrate.

TWENTY-SIX

Matilda Shawcross, the head teacher of St Jude's Catholic Junior School, stood up from behind her desk as DI Snow and DS Fellows were shown into the office by a rather flustered secretary.

'I must confess that I had not expected to see the gentlemen of the police so soon … after last time,' she said as she waved them to two chairs opposite her. She looked, thought Snow, remarkably young to be in such an elevated position in the academic world. To him her self-assurance, sleek figure, fine skin and bright eyes were those of a woman only just entering her thirties. She was attractive, self-contained and intelligent. Snow liked her immediately. She was dressed in a smart black suit and a fine white shirt. Her fair hair was cut short in a gamine style, giving emphasis to her high cheekbones and large grey eyes. To his surprise, Snow found her strangely alluring. It disturbed him slightly that he was taking in so much of her appearance and not concentrating fully on the purpose of the visit.

'I presume there is no further news about poor Elizabeth,' she said.

Snow shook his head. 'I am afraid not, but in circumstances like this it is sometimes good not to have any news.'

The head teacher gave an understanding nod. 'So, how can I be of assistance?'

'We believe that Elizabeth has been taken …'

'What! I knew that she was missing – but kidnapped … again?' Her grey eyes widened in surprise. 'I thought you had arrested the man who took her?'

'Yes. We suspect that this is a completely different individual.'

'My God. Are you sure?'

'We are not sure of anything at the moment. We are trying to piece things together.'

'Of course.' Matilda Shawcross shook her head in disbelief at the news she had just received. 'What a nightmare. How may I help?'

'I am just hoping that one of your students may have seen something. At the end of school yesterday.'

'I really don't know.'

'What I'd like to do is speak to your students in morning assembly to see if I can jog someone's memory. You still have morning assemblies, I assume.'

'Of course. This is a Catholic school. We have a hymn, prayers and a moralistic tale.'

'I'd appreciate your co-operation in this.'

'I understand, Inspector. However …' She paused, thinking how she could frame her thoughts, before continuing. 'I am sure you are aware of the sensitivity of such an exercise. These are young, impressionable girls. I would be neglecting my duty if I allowed them to be frightened or upset by what you are going to say.'

'Of course. I understand. Don't worry, I won't be raising any bogeymen or stimulating any nasty dreams. I just want to know if any of your girls saw Elizabeth at the end of the day and if they saw anything unusual. I will tread carefully, believe me.'

The head gave a taut but pleasant smile. 'Very well, I will arrange it. If there is anyone with information that might help they can come to my room immediately after assembly where you can have a chat with them.'

'That would be good. Thank you.'

She glanced at her watch. 'Assembly is in three-quarters of an hour. Would you like a cup of tea while you wait?'

Snow was surprised how nervous he became when it was his turn to stand up in front of two hundred young girls to deliver his spiel. Miss Shawcross had introduced him as Mr Snow, an important policeman, and as he stood at the front of the stage in the school hall to address the girls he suddenly found his mouth going dry. It wasn't the best of performances, he thought afterwards, but he managed to convey the main points in a tone that was appropriate and the head seemed pleased with his tact and restraint.

They did not have long to wait after the assembly had taken place before someone came knocking at the head teacher's door. She ushered in two ten-year-olds whom she introduced to Snow as Mary Fields and Cathy Newbould.

'You have something to tell Mr Snow? Something about Elizabeth?'

The girls nodded mutely.

'There's no need to be frightened,' said Snow gently, kneeling so that his face was on their level. 'Just tell me what you know.'

The two girls exchanged glances and then Mary jabbed Cathy gently in the ribs to respond. 'We were with Lizzie at the end of school – in the yard – when the policeman arrived to see her,' she said.

'The policeman?' came the surprised response from Bob Fellows.

The girls flinched at this outburst. Snow ignored it and carried on gently. 'How do you know it was a policeman?' he asked.

''Cause he had one of them blue uniforms on,' said Cathy.

'Yes, I think he had three stripes on his arm,' added her friend.

'A sergeant,' suggested Snow.

The girls nodded.

'What did this policeman say to Elizabeth – Lizzie?'

'He said her mum had been involved in a car accident – a crash or something – and he'd come to take Lizzie to the hospital to see her. He said she was not to worry. Her mum was going to be all right.'

'What did Lizzie do when he told her this?'

'Well,' said Cathy, 'at first she started to cry a bit and we gave her a hug, but the policeman said there wasn't time to hang about. They ought to be off.'

'He took her hand and led her away,' said Mary.

'Did you see the car they got into?'

The girls shook their heads.

'What did this policeman look like?'

The two friends wrinkled their noses and exchanged glances. 'Sort of ordinary, really,' ventured Cathy.

'Did he look like me, for instance?' asked Snow, standing up so they could get a good look at him.

'About as tall. Oh, he had blond hair.'

'His nose was a bit big,' said Mary, giggling.

'Was he fat or thin?'

'He was quite thin and his voice was a bit croaky.'

'Anything else?'

They paused and then both shook their heads.

'Thank you, girls. You have been a great help.' Snow gave them a brief smile.

'Best get back to your class now,' said Miss Shawcross, moving to the door and opening it for them. Just before they left, Mary turned to Snow. 'Is Lizzie OK? How's her mum?' she asked.

The policeman was a little perplexed as to how to reply to this query. He couldn't tell them the truth and yet he did not want to upset the youngsters or prompt them to start rumours amongst their classmates.

It was Miss Shawcross who came to Snow's rescue. 'There have been some misunderstandings which have led to a few complications that these police officers are trying to sort out,' she said smiling. 'There is nothing to worry about. Truly.'

'Thank you,' said Snow when the girls had departed.

Matilda Shawcross flashed Snow a warm smile. 'Reassuring students comes as second nature in my job, Inspector. Most children are eager to be told all is well and they accept that confirmation without much soul-searching.' Her smile broadened.

For a moment, Snow was caught by that smile and those bright, intelligent eyes. He felt strange and unnerved, for he realised that he was in some odd way drawn to her. He never felt this way about women. Sensually they barely registered on his radar. Now he felt uncomfortable and tongue-tied. His cheeks began to burn and suddenly the collar of his shirt seemed too tight.

'Thank you … thank you for your help,' he managed to stammer.

'I hope it has been of help,' she said, touching his arm in a solicitous fashion. 'I know how difficult this must be for you. I don't envy you your job. Please let me know if you have any news of Elizabeth. It must be a most worrying time for her parents.'

'I will.' Snow moved to the door awkwardly and collided with Bob Fellows.

'You all right, sir?' asked Fellows, as they walked from the school to their car.

'Yes, of course.'

'It's just that you looked a bit flummoxed in the head's office at the end. You seemed to dry up.'

'Did I?' The tone that Snow used was signal enough to Bob Fellows to drop the subject.

'So it looks like we have some sort of copycat killer on the job,' he said, moving on to firmer ground.

'Well, I am convinced that there is no direct connection between Hirst and this new fellow. He's come out of the blue, working on his own. But why? What on earth is his motive?'

'To finish the job that Hirst started.'

'Possibly. That would be the obvious answer. But there is something more, I'm convinced of it.'

'What?'

'That I don't know.'

'What now?'

'Back to base, I guess. We'll need to check once again on those who had relatives involved in that coach crash. Particularly those who are male, tallish with blond hair and a prominent nose. I'll get on with that and you see what you can find out about the sergeant's uniform. Check if any have gone missing. It's also quite possible that he hired one from a stage costume place. There's a couple locally and a big one in Leeds. Get Susan to help you to follow that one up.'

Bob nodded. 'Of course, there is another possibility.'

Snow nodded. 'I know. That he used his own …'

As Snow busied himself, or tried to busy himself, with the routine business of following up the frail leads that this incident had presented, he found his mind allowing strange and preposterous ideas to leak into his consciousness concerning the abduction of Elizabeth Saunders. There was something far more challenging, far more unnerving about this crime. The fact that his name had been mentioned by the perpetrator made it very personal and it seemed to him, although he could hardly admit the thought, let alone verbalise it, that the girl had been taken as a punishment for him. To cause him pain and distress. He tried to block this idea, but with a fierce relentlessness, it returned to haunt him.

He had succeeded in keeping the story from the press. In this case, publicity would be detrimental rather than helpful. He also organised police surveillance on Teresa Duff, the other survivor of the coach crash. He was fairly certain she would be targeted before long. He prayed that this was some kind of sick game and the man who had taken Elizabeth did not really intend to kill her. Just to teach him a lesson … God, there was that thought again.

At the end of a long, weary day, Snow sat in his office, tense and drained. Bob Fellows had reported that there was no one directly connected with the coach crash who was tall with blond hair and a big nose. Similarly, there had been a dead end in the police uniform enquiries. This particularly increased Snow's angst because it allowed him to consider that the abductor had worn his *own* uniform, that he was in fact a policeman. Not only did that slice the lid off a particularly nasty can of worms but it was another tick on the checklist of the nightmarish theory that was building in his mind, one that would not go away.

As dusk began to fall, he gave in to it and decided to carry out a basic investigation, one which, with any luck, would kick these dark ideas into touch. After making a few telephone enquiries, he headed out of town towards Brighouse, a small town some five miles from Huddersfield. As the road dropped down from the Fixby roundabout, he made a sharp left and turned into Tinker Lane. Although it was just off the busy main road, it was a leafy and very suburban thoroughfare with the houses shielded by trees and high walls. He parked the car and made his way until he reached number 17, a fifties bungalow, with a neat but boring garden. There was a small driveway at the side of the building, leading to a single garage. There were no lights on in the house.

Snow went through the routine of ringing the doorbell, fairly sure that no one would answer. That proved to be the case. He skirted along the front of the house, across the lawn, and peered in at the sitting-room window. It was very difficult to make anything out but it was clear that the house was empty. He slipped around to the back of the property and gained entry by the kitchen door. With speed and efficiency, he visited every room in the house, giving it a cursory once-over, hoping that something would easily identify itself as a useful clue. Nothing did. All was neat and tidy and devoid of any clues. That was until he visited the bedroom. There on the candlewick bedspread was a foolscap envelope bearing his name.

Snow's heart constricted when he saw it. He stared at the envelope for over a minute, not daring to touch it, almost as though he thought it would burst into flames if he did so. Eventually, he leaned forward, took up the envelope and slowly pulled back the loose flap to extract the content, which was one single sheet of A4 paper with writing in a red felt-tip pen: 'Catch Me If You Can.'

Snow closed his eyes in horror. So he had been right. That very nasty theory that had been nagging him all day was the correct one. The man he was after was Colin Bird. Colin Bird, the tall chap with blond hair and a prominent nose. It was crazy! He was the one who had taken Elizabeth Saunders, apparently carrying on where Frank Hirst had left off. But why? Could it be that all this was because Snow had rejected his advances? A lover spurned had taken a young girl in bitter spite and had untied the knot of Snow's successful murder case.

'The man must be mad,' muttered Snow to himself as he gazed once more at the taunting message. Mad? Indeed, but that didn't help matters. It made them far worse. Where there was madness, there was no logic. Only the corkscrew kind.

Snow stuffed the note in his inside pocket and made his way downstairs. He realised that, now he was sure Bird was behind the abduction, he couldn't keep the matter to himself any more. How on earth would it look to his colleagues? What light did it shine on him? Why would a gay man make advances to DI Paul Snow? How could he explain that? With difficulty. He swore. That was a bridge he would have to cross at some point …

However, the real big question now was – where the hell was Bird hiding out? Snow realised that a more rigorous search of the house was necessary to see if he could dig up any clues as to where Bird was. For the next forty minutes or so he did a fine sweep of the premises: checking drawers, cupboards, shelves and clothing in a desperate attempt to find something, any little something, that might give a clue to Bird's plans or whereabouts. He even emptied out an old golfing bag, but to no avail. As he grew more and more frustrated, it occurred to Snow that Bird, an experienced copper like himself, had preceded him and removed anything which might be of use to those on his tail. That was until he examined the contents of the pedal bin in the kitchen.

Towards the bottom of the bin, amongst some gooey detritus, were a couple of scraps of paper from a formal letter. They had been screwed up into a tight ball. There was no sign of the remaining section of the letter, but as Snow unfurled these scraps and read them, he experienced a flicker of hope. They were part of a communication from Silver Trees Country Cottages and it would seem Mr Bird was hiring one of their properties for a month. There was a reference number and a name of the cottage, which was Links View. The location was not given but the date of the communication was only four days ago.

Then he remembered there had been a brochure in the magazine rack from Silver Trees which he had ignored. He moved swiftly into the sitting room, retrieved the brochure and sat down to examine it carefully. It didn't take him long to find Links View Cottage. It was located, as he assumed, near a golf course; this one was on the outskirts of Meltham, a village just eight miles from the centre of Huddersfield, heading towards the Lancashire border. The bastard wanted to remain at the centre of the action, thought Snow, a grim smile touching his features briefly.

Now he had to decide what do to. Should he turn vigilante and thus reduce the possibility of the fallout from Bird's motives, which would certainly place him, Snow, firmly under scrutiny and possibly lead to his exposure? Or should he inform his colleagues and turn it into an authorised operation?

He sat in the gloom for five minutes or so, agonising over what to do. Eventually, with a sigh, he rose from his chair and made for the door. He had made his decision and he wanted to act quickly before he changed his mind. As he left the house and headed for his car, he hoped to God he was doing the right thing.

TWENTY-SEVEN

It took Snow about forty minutes to drive from Brighouse to the village of Meltham. He called in at the Waggon and Horses, one of the four public houses in the village, and, over half a pint, enquired of the young barman where the golf club was situated and, in particular, if he knew where Links View Cottage was.

The lad shook his head. 'I'm not from round here. I'm a student at the Poly. This is my night job to help pay my way. Sorry, mate.'

'Maybe I can help,' chipped in a ruddy-faced fellow, perched on a stool by the bar. He was the epitome of a country gent who had seen better days. His expensive tweed jacket was faded, pilled and had lost its shape and, thought Snow, the will to remain a jacket any more. The fellow wore a woollen waistcoat, complete with a series of holes, a checked shirt with curling collar and a shabby yellow tie. His nose was red and richly veined, the effect of nights by the bar rather than the bracing Yorkshire weather.

Snow smiled. 'That would be kind,' he replied.

The ruddy-faced fellow placed his empty whisky glass on the counter close to Snow and gazed at it with a rheumy sadness.

'Perhaps I could buy you a drink,' said Snow, quickly picking up the unashamed hint.

'You certainly may. It will give me time to get my brain clear to give you directions to Links View Cottage.'

'You know it?' asked Snow, as he pointed to the empty whisky glass, indicating that the barman should replenish it.

'God, yes. When Adam was a boy, I used to be a big noise up at the golf club and we had that place for parties. We had some nights there, I can tell you. That was before the committee saw fit to turn it into a bloody rented place for the townies to rest their weary limbs. It helped the club coffers, I suppose, but it was a damned shame that we lost a party venue. I say, you're not one of those townies, are you?'

Snow shook his head and put on a smile. 'No, I'm a local lad. I'm just visiting a friend up there. He comes from this neck of the woods as well.'

The old fellow nodded and took another sip of his scotch.

'Where exactly is it?' prompted Snow.

His companion raised his glass and took another generous gulp. 'You in a motor?' he said when he had savoured the alcohol.

'Yes.'

'Then it's easy peasy. Turn left at the end of the street here, go up Wessenden Head Road and when the road forks in about a mile, go left again and within five minutes you are on the perimeter of the golf course. It's a lovely one, you know. Fantastic views. Very bracing. You a golfer?'

'No, no.'

'Really. That's a damned pity.'

'What then?'

'Turn in at the main entrance of the club, tootle down the drive for about half a mile and you'll see a dirt track off to the left. Go down there until you see it. There's a small pool nearby so don't run the old jalopy into it, eh.' He chuckled, overly amused at his own observation.

'Thank you.' Snow made to move when the old fellow touched his elbow.

'You're not going now, are you?'

'Yes.'

'Damn pity. I was hoping to keep you talking a little while longer. You see my glass is nearly empty again.' At this he roared with laughter.

'Maybe next time,' said Snow, beating a hasty retreat.

Snow followed the old fellow's directions and within ten minutes he was making his way down the very long sweeping drive of Holme Valley Golf Club, which ran through the gently undulating fairways. Far away on his right he could see the twinkling lights of Holmfirth and some scattered cottages in the hills beyond. About a mile ahead of him was the silhouette of the golf house itself, ghostly against the mid blue of the evening sky. Passing through a little copse, he saw the dirt road off to the left. He drove down it a while until he caught sight in the distance of the outline of a low building which he assumed was Links View Cottage. There was no glow from the windows suggesting habitation. It stood stark and strangely foreboding, in relief against the night sky.

Snow pulled his car into the side of the track, close to a bank of bushes. He switched off the engine and lights and stared out into the darkness. So, here he was. There was no real going back now. He waited a few moments, staring at the dark building, willing it to somehow reveal its secrets. Was Colin Bird holed up in there? Is this where he had taken the girl? Was she still alive? As that question filtered into his brain, he felt his throat constrict. He wasn't a religious man so he could not pray that the girl was all right, unharmed or still alive at least. But he willed it with as much inner force as he could muster.

Still those questions ricocheted around his brain. Questions, questions, questions! The only way to find the answers to those was to act. With a deep intake of breath, he left the car and, keeping to the shadows, began making his way towards the cottage.

He moved towards the copse which surrounded the far side of the pool. From here, moving to his right, he could see the front of the cottage which had a small American-style wooden porch with an upholstered bench that afforded a view of the pool. Snow realised that he would have to break cover and skirt the pool in order to approach the front door. Fleetingly, he contemplated moving to the extreme right of the copse and slipping down the far side of the cottage to see if there was anywhere he could gain entry from the rear. While he was considering this notion, he heard a rustling sound in the bushes behind him. As he turned slowly, it seemed a very bright light, like a flash of lightning, dazzled him. This coincided with him experiencing a sudden fierce pain in the side of the head. He had just seconds to realise that he had been slugged hard, before his legs gave way and he lost consciousness.

TWENTY-EIGHT

The first thing that Snow became conscious of before he opened his eyes was the sound of music and the smell of marijuana. He kept his eyes closed while he waited for all his other senses to reassert themselves. It didn't take him long to realise that he had a pounding headache and the side of his head throbbed painfully. Then he remembered the blow. The memory of it strangely seemed to increase the pain that he felt. Breathing gently to help stabilise his nerves and heart rate, while still keeping the eyes shut, he tried to estimate what kind of situation he was in. Quite quickly he was able to ascertain that his arms were tied behind his back. The bonds were tight and chafing his wrists, but his feet were free. He was lying face downwards on some sort of rough rug or floor covering. He thought he recognised the music. It was scratchy and old, some French tune which was played, he was fairly certain, by Stéphane Grappelli and Django Reinhardt. He almost smiled, aware how inconsequential the identification of the music was to his current predicament, which he now assessed as being very dangerous indeed. It would seem that he had been caught by Colin Bird, who had trussed him up and dragged him into the cottage and was no doubt sitting close by with a drink, smoking a spliff and listening to jazz while he waited for DI Paul Snow to regain consciousness so that he could … what? Torment him? Kill him?

Slowly, he opened his eyes and tried to bring things into focus. His first sight was of two large, brown suede shoes and the bottoms of some tan trousers. Gently raising his neck and twisting his head slightly, he saw that they belonged to Colin Bird who was sitting in an armchair, leaning forward, with a thin cigarette dangling from his lips, gazing at him through a net of fine spirals of grey smoke.

'So, back with us, eh, Pauley. Good to see you again.' The voice was gentle, friendly even, but rich in sarcasm.

'I'd like to sit upright,' said Snow simply.

'Certainly,' came the reply and Bird left his seat and hauled Paul into a sitting position, resting him against the corresponding armchair across from his own.

'It is so fortunate that you are a man of habit. A man with a predictable streak. Easy to assess. Easy to track down. You never did catch on that our encounter in the supermarket was no coincidence, did you?'

'Of course. I recognise a stalker when I see one.'

Bird shrugged. 'Maybe, but it was so simple for me to turn up there to encounter Mr Regular who shops for his food twice a week on Thursdays and Mondays around seven in the evening. I have studied you, my friend. Got to know all your little ways. Your likes and dislikes. Even your taste in music.' He waved his hand in the air. 'The Hot Club of Paris. Playing especially for you. Stéphane and Django.'

Bird leant down and planted a kiss on Snow's forehead. 'I know you, Paul Snow. Intimately. Well, in one sense of that word. You put a stop to the other sense.'

'It was nothing personal.'

Bird ignored the remark. 'That's how I knew you would be the perfect lover, if only … if only you had enough courage to be true to yourself. To be, as our Jewish friends say, to be a mensch. You live in a strait-jacket and it will destroy you in the end.'

Bird leaned back and picked up a glass from a small table by his seat. It was filled with what Paul assumed was whisky. Bird downed it in one gulp and shuddered as he did so.

'Yes, I know my Pauley,' he resumed. 'That's why I was able to lure you here.'

'Lure me?'

Bird laughed. It was a genuine, hearty laugh. 'Yes. I set a kind of trap for you. A trail for you to follow. You don't think you've suddenly become Sherlock Holmes, do you? Picking up clues, making deductions and tracing Professor Moriarty to his secret lair?' He laughed again. 'Actually, I think you do. Well, think again, Sherlock. I set you up! You see, I knew you would visit my house and give it the once-over – the special Snow search. I needed to leave you something there to draw you to me.'

A chill finger stroked Snow's spine. 'The invoices in the bin …' It was almost a whisper – a whisper to himself. Snow bit his lip with frustration. He had been well and truly fooled.

Bird was laughing again. 'As I was placing them in the bin, making sure one was smeared with baked bean sauce, I couldn't help but smile as I saw you in my mind's eye, finding them and thinking "Bingo, I've got him." Unfortunately, the reverse applies: Bingo, I've got you.'

'And what about the girl?'

'What girl?'

'You know damn well which girl. Where is she? Have you harmed her?'

'Now that would be telling.'

'Colin, think, for goodness' sake. You've been foolish and you won't get away with this, but if you add murder to kidnap …'

'Oh, I know all about that. I'll end up in a nasty cell and be spat at and beaten up by loads of unpleasant folk and never walk the streets again. You never know my luck; I might get buggered inside as well.'

Bird's eyes rolled wildly now and Snow could see that the man's slide into madness was exacerbated by his intake of marijuana and alcohol. In this growing state of instability there was no telling what the mad bastard would do.

'Let me help you, Colin. The situation is not hopeless.'

'Help me? How the bloody hell are you going to help me?'

'We could work it out. If the girl is alive, we can sort it. You're right, I do live in a straitjacket. Perhaps now it's time to take the thing off.'

Bird sneered broadly at first and then his features darkened. 'A bit late in the day for that, Pauley.'

Snow shook his head. 'No, no. You're right. I see that now. Let me be a mensch.'

'You don't think I'm going to fall for this particular line of bluff taking, do you?'

'You've got to listen to me. I'm serious and honest. Come on, Colin, I'm your only hope. Just as long as the girl is all right.'

'The girl! The fucking girl! That's all you're worried about, isn't it? Let's save the brat and to hell with me then.'

Snow shook his head. 'You're missing the point, Colin. The girl is the key. If she's unharmed, I can work this, I can work this for both of us. Remember, at the moment I'm the only one who is on to you. If we can return the girl to her family, it will be relatively easy to cover up the traces. You need never figure in the matter.'

'And why would you do that? Why would you do that for me?'

'The truth?'

'The truth!'

'To save the girl's life – and to give you a chance. To give us a chance.'

'Us.'

'Yes, you and me. You have made me see how … wrong I've been in my attitude to my sexuality. It is possible…'

'Now … now you say this. Now, when it's too late.'

'Too late? What do you mean? The girl …'

'I don't mean the girl anything. I mean us. How could we get together after all this? How could we trust each other?'

'We'd have to learn. Time would help. Soon this could just be a bad memory.'

Bird shook his head. 'No, no, it's gone too far.'

'Not yet it hasn't – but what's the alternative to my suggestion? Are you going to kill me and that innocent little girl just out of spite, fury? Just because you can't get your own way? That way madness lies.'

Colin Bird gazed at Snow for some moments, his moist features trembling, and then he sank back in the chair with a groan. He dropped the spliff in an ashtray and covered his face with his hands. Paul could not tell if he was crying or not. His body was shaking with emotion, whether it was with despair or twisted amusement, it was difficult to say. Whatever, Paul knew that he couldn't sit quietly and wait for Bird to make his own mind up about things. He had to persevere, persuade, cajole, bring the crazy bastard around to his way of thinking.

'Stop it now, Colin. Untie me and we can start to make things right. I can help you, you know that.'

Bird let out a roar and rose from the chair, waving his arms wildly in the air. His face was damp with tears. 'I don't know. I don't know,' he bellowed, staggering forward a few steps before slumping backwards into the chair once more. 'I should stick to my plan. I should,' he said suddenly, all emotion draining from his face. 'Yeah, yeah, I'm gonna stick to my plan. I've thought the whole thing through. Worked out the details carefully, meticulously. It would be foolish to abandon it now. I'm sorry, Paul, but I can't trust you. You say one thing now, but if I let you go free, how do I know you won't turn on me again? Reject me. Try to get me arrested. Sent down for life.'

Snow shook his head violently. 'No, Colin, I won't. We can be together. We can work it out. Trust me!'

'No! No! I don't trust you. The time for talking is over. I need to kill you and then the girl.' He shrugged his shoulders almost in a kind of apologetic gesture. 'You see,' he said softly, 'I've got to stick to my plan.'

TWENTY-NINE

In the small bedroom at the back of the cottage, Colin Bird's strident voice had roused Elizabeth Saunders from her drugged slumber. At first she stirred uneasily and her eyes opened wide, the pupils slowly adjusting to the gloom. With some effort she pulled herself up into a sitting position and waited for her vision to stabilise. A feeble flickering nightlight on the bedside table revealed that she was in a small bedroom.

It was not her own.

This fact distressed her, as did the sudden realisation that her hands were tied together in front of her with thin rope. How did that happen? Who did that to her?

Her worried puzzlement grew as her brain cleared. She had no idea where she was or how she had got here. She tried hard to remember and then slowly images emerged in her mind, as through a fog. Her memory began to reform. There she was with her friends Mary and Cathy, leaving school and … Yes, it was coming back to her now. There was the policeman who had approached them. He was a tall man. He had a large nose. She saw his face swim before her in her mind's eye. He said something to her. He said he had come to collect her. Why was that? What did he want? Oh, yes, her mother. She had been in an accident … At this thought, Elizabeth's heart began beating faster.

'Mummy,' she whispered, a tear forming in her eyes. But then another thought struck her. The policeman had kidnapped her – like that first man. She had got in the car with him but he had stopped a few streets away and placed a cloth over her face. She had tried to struggle but he had been too strong for her.

Yes, he had kidnapped her. There was nothing wrong with her mother. She wasn't in hospital at all. That was all a story. A story to fool her, to get her to go along with the man. The man in the policeman's uniform. I bet he wasn't a policeman at all. He just wore a uniform like one. No, he wasn't a policeman – he was … She gasped out loud and her whole body trembled as she uttered the words to herself in a grating whisper: 'he was a murderer.' Like that first man, he meant to kill her.

Panic now set in and with a sudden desperate movement she tried to get off the bed. She fell with a thump on to the floor. The shock of this actually cleared her brain even more. The dreamlike quality of her experience had disappeared entirely and was replaced with a brutal and frightening reality. With difficulty, she scrambled to her feet. She knew she had to escape. She knew her life was in danger and she needed to get away before …

She moved to the door and although she tried the handle she knew in her heart that it would be locked. With both hands she grasped the handle and turned. It twisted easily but the door did not move.

It was locked.

She knelt down and looked through the keyhole. The key was in there at the other side of the door. After a moment's thought, she knew what she must do. Act like Simon Templar. The Saint. She had seen him get out of a locked room in one of his TV shows. It was a simple trick. If only it would work for her. Raising both her arms, she managed to extract one of the hairpins from her hair and then carefully she bent and twisted it into a sturdy single length. Satisfied that she had she the best she could with the straightened hairpin, she approached the door once more and then poked it firmly through the aperture of the keyhole. It soon met with the obstruction of the key on the other side. With her eye pressed as close to the keyhole as possible, Elizabeth attempted to turn the end of the key straight. At first it resisted, but with further prodding, it began to move. After less than a minute, it looked to her as though she had straightened the key in the lock. A brief smile lit her face.

Dragging the flimsy bedside mat to the door, she slipped it through the gap at the bottom so that half of it was now outside the room. Now came the dangerous and difficult bit. It had worked for the Saint but he was on television and, on reflection, Elizabeth realised that it could easily have been a special effect. With her tongue protruding from the corner of her mouth as she concentrated, she thrust the twisted hairpin with great vigour hard against the end of the key. Remarkably, with one blow the key moved, slipping backwards, almost to the end of the aperture but not quite. Elizabeth's tummy was now vibrating with excitement and anticipation. One more thrust, she thought, would do it. She was right. Her second attempt dislodged the key and, with a small thud, it landed on the floor on the other side of the door. Gingerly, Elizabeth pulled the mat back. The key got stuck half way under the door but she was able to drag it through with her fingers. She beamed as she held the small metal implement. It was not only the key to the bedroom, but, as she saw it, her key to freedom.

Colin Bird towered over Snow and the policeman could tell by looking at his eyes that his captor had lost it completely. Any shred of reason or rationality that had existed in his fragile brain had gone. For a time he seemed to have been persuaded by Snow's entreaties, but then something had snapped inside his head and any effect that the words, persuasions and encouragements may have had on him before were useless now. He had slipped into mania and there would be no reasoning with him.

With a grunt of satisfaction, Bird leaned forward slowly, his face muscles twitching erratically while his hands reached out for Snow's neck. In response, Snow edged away in a desperate attempt to escape, moving backwards, shuffling along the carpet, while trying hard to jerk himself up into a sitting position. But Bird continued to follow and then Snow reached as far back as he could go, trapped up against the armchair. His attacker chuckled, flexing his fingers once more, ready for the kill.

In desperation, Snow kicked upwards with his right leg with as much force as he could muster, his foot catching Bird hard in the crotch. He gave a groan, his hands flying to the injured area and, staggering sideways, he slipped down on to the floor.

In an instant Snow managed to drag himself to his feet and let loose with his foot once more. This time the target was Bird's face. The toe of his shoe smashed his captor in the mouth. Bird cried out in pain and anger as blood spurted over his teeth in a fine red shower and began to dribble down his chin. However, Snow could see that this was a hollow victory, for while he had obviously hurt his opponent, this had only further fuelled his anger. Like a creature on fire, Bird jumped to his feet and hurled himself at Snow, his fingers latching themselves firmly around his throat. The two men crashed backwards on to the floor, with Bird on top of Snow, the blood from his wound dripping on to the policeman's face.

'I'm sticking to my plan!' Bird exclaimed wildly, as his fingers pressed harder against Snow's windpipe. He struggled in vain, but the weight of Bird on him and the fierce pressure that he was applying to his throat made it impossible for him to move. Strangely, as sometimes happens in moments of great danger, Snow suddenly felt a moment of calm. It struck him quite simply that this was it. This was where his life was about to end. Already the flow of precious oxygen to his brain was being severely restricted and he hadn't the strength to dislodge this bloody murderer. Already a thin, grey curtain seemed to be forming before his eyes. Yes, he thought, with a strange feeling of acceptance, I am going to die.

THIRTY

Once Elizabeth had escaped from her bedroom prison, as she thought of it, her bravado deserted her. It was as though she had suddenly realised the full, fierce reality of her desperate situation. She stood still in the darkness outside the bedroom, wondering what to do next. There were loud noises coming from the room at the far end of the corridor. It sounded as though someone was having a violent argument: voices were raised, sharp cries reverberated in the air and there was the crashing of furniture.

Curiosity got the better of her caution and she tiptoed down the corridor; with some trepidation she opened the door a fraction and peered through the crack into the room beyond. She saw two men fighting, growling and roaring at each other. One of them was the blond man she knew. The policeman with the big nose. The man who had kidnapped her. The one who had lied and told her that her mother was ill in hospital.

He was a bad man.

To her chagrin, this bad man seemed to be winning the fight. She didn't know who the other person was. She couldn't see his face properly, but she assumed, if he was being attacked by Mr Big Nose, he must be the goody in the situation. Instinctively she knew she had to save him. He might be able to help her to escape. If Mr Big Nose won, he would capture her again. This terrible thought prompted her action.

She moved quietly into the room while the two men continued to tussle with each other. They crashed to the ground, Mr Big Nose landing on top of the other. He gave a strange gurgling cry and bellowed, 'I'm sticking to my plan!'

She saw to her horror that Mr Big Nose had his large hands around the other man's throat and was throttling him to death. The victim's face had gone a bright pink and the eyes began to flicker and close. She had to stop him. She had to stop him killing that man. In wild desperation, she gazed around and her eyes lit upon a whisky bottle on the sideboard. She rushed forward and snatched it up.

Her movement caught Bird's attention and for a brief moment he froze and turned his head in the girl's direction. He saw her advancing towards him with the bottle raised.

'You,' he cried, before the first blow was struck. It came down hard against his temple and knocked him forward so that he fell limply on to the man on the floor.

Snow was only vaguely aware of what was happening now. Bird's fingers loosened around his neck and he was able to gasp for air. As Snow looked up, he saw a trickle of blood appear at the side of Bird's head and run through the fine blond hairs on to his face.

The sight of the shiny red blood somehow seemed to enrage the girl. It brought her visions of the man leering over her when she had been imprisoned in that bedroom. He meant to harm her. She knew that instinctively. Now it was her chance to harm him. She hit him again.

And again.

Snow was now able to disentangle himself from Bird's limp embrace and, pulling himself up into a sitting position, he quickly assessed the situation. The girl had gone wild as if in some sort of fit, raining a series of blows upon the now unconscious Bird.

'Stop it!' Snow's voice emerged croaky and faint. He tried again and this time he was able to increase the volume. 'Please, stop it. Put the bottle down,' he cried. But his words had no effect. Elizabeth did not seem to hear him. It was as though she was now in a world of her own. She brought the bottle crashing down on Bird's skull yet again.

Snow, his hands still bound, struggled to pull himself forward towards her. 'No, no. Stop it.' But the girl, her eyes glazed and her mouth set in a fanatical rictus grin, was now possessed and without seeming to see clearly she brought the bottle down once more. This time it connected with the side of Snow's head instead. He gave out a yelp of pain and the shock blocked his vision with a fierce white light. When the mist cleared, he saw the bottle descend once more. There was nothing he could do to avoid the blow. He was briefly aware of the violent pain it brought him before he blacked out completely.

THIRTY-ONE

A strange rustling noise came to his ears but what was causing it he couldn't say. That was partly because he was in darkness. But he liked being in darkness. It was safe and secure here. Something told him that in the light there would be more pain – more pain than he was feeling now. The pain that made him feel as though his head was on fire or people were drilling holes his brain. No, he thought, I'll stay in the darkness. I won't open my eyes. I'll just go back to sleep. I'll be safe here.

And as he drifted off to sleep once more, the rustling sound faded.

Without planning it, or giving it any thought, instinctively he opened his eyes. If he had had chance to consider this action, he would have kept them shut, remained in the security of the dark. But his body had taken the decision to bring him back.

The eyelids fluttered, allowing the light in slowly. It was painful at first, making his eyes water, which helped to increase his blurred vision. He took several deep breaths as he tried to make sense of it all. Where was he? Who was he and what was happening to him? And why did his head hurt so?

Soon, he was able to determine that he was lying in a bed. A very soft and comfortable bed with smooth sheets that rustled at his slightest movement. He gazed above him at the ceiling. It was one he did not recognise. It was plain white with a few fine, spidery cracks in it and a hanging light fitting with a long fluorescent tube. Now, he thought, he must be brave and pull himself up in the bed and try to see where he was. But he couldn't, he was too weak.

Suddenly a woman's face appeared close to his. So close that he could see the pores and touches of make-up on her cheeks. Her face somehow seemed very large. The red lips – which parted in a gentle smile – seemed like those of a giant. He blinked to reassess this vision.

'So you've decided to come back and join us.' The giant lips moved, forming these words.

He could not respond to this. He was not sure what it meant or who this oversized woman was.

'Let's give you a sip of water. Lubricate your throat.' She held a paper cup to his dry, cracked lips and allowed the water to pass through. It felt so good. Snow leaned forward a little, greedily slurping in the liquid. It was the best drink in the world.

'There's a good boy.'

Snow peered up at her again. Of course, she was a nurse. She was looking after him. He must be ill.

With these simple thoughts in his mind, he slipped back into sleep.

When he woke again, it was dark in the room. The fluorescent tube above his bed was not lit and the nurse was not there. For a moment he felt a sense of panic, but his tired and damaged mind gradually came to the rescue. Memory began to form in his head like a tattered jigsaw puzzle. Slowly he remembered the closing moments of his life before darkness descended. As he did so, he became conscious of the dull pain in his head and the tight bandage that encased it.

He had been knocked unconscious; knocked senseless, concussed. That was it. He smiled at the deduction. He was in hospital and in safe hands.

Well, I am still alive but I hurt like hell, he thought.

Slowly and gingerly, he pulled himself from his prone position so that he could see the room a little better.

'Hello!' he called out. His voice strange, rough and alien. 'Hello,' he called again.

The door opened and a dark face peered into the room. 'Hello, nuisance,' it said brightly.

'Could I have a cup of coffee, please?'

The Jamaican nurse chuckled. 'Of course you can, darlin'. How do you like it?'

'Black and strong.'

'Like me, you mean.' She laughed. 'Coming right up and seeing that you've been a good boy I'll see if I can get you a couple of chocolate biscuits.'

'Thank you,' said Snow, sinking down in the bed again, feeling as though he'd done a day's work.

The next morning he was visited by a doctor after he had managed to consume a simple scrambled egg breakfast. The doctor conducted a few tests, asking Snow to tell him how many fingers he was holding up, reading aloud from a sheet and carefully following the trajectory of his Biro.

'You seem to be on the mend all right, but the old bonce has taken quite a bashing, you know,' said the young medic, sitting on the edge of Snow's bed. 'You've been badly concussed and it will take a while before you'll feel your old self again. You'll need to rest for a few weeks before you can get back in the saddle. The brain is a delicate organ, you know, and will take a while to fully recuperate. Don't try and rush things or you can cause yourself some problems.'

'I understand. When can I leave?'

The doctor smiled. 'Not so fast. You're not ready yet. A couple of days, I reckon, but we'll need to give that brain of yours a scan first. Just to make absolutely certain there's no permanent damage. In the meantime it's your job to relax and take advantage of the rest. Can't tell you what I'd give for a couple of days in bed being looked after by a set of pretty nurses.'

With a laugh and a cheery wave he left.

In the afternoon, Paul Snow had a visitor. He woke for his post-lunch nap to find Bob Fellows sitting patiently on a chair by his bedside. He was never more pleased to see the bulky form and ruddy cheeks of his DS. He was a link with the outside world, his old life and, for want of a better word, reality.

Bob grinned. 'Good to see you, sir, although I must admit I've seen you looking better.'

'Somewhat ropey, eh?'

Bob nodded. 'A bit like a Picasso painting. Your face is a mass of colours from blues to red to yellow. And your nose seems a little bent. Still the doc seems pleased with your progress.'

'That's good.'

'I would have brought you grapes but …'

Snow laughed heartily, although his head ached as he did so. 'I'm not really interested in grapes. But what I am interested in is … the story.'

'The story?'

'How did I get here? What's happened to Bird and the little girl?'

'Are you sure you're up to all that?'

'Of course I am. It will comfort me to have those pieces put into place.'

'Well, there are certain pieces missing from my end too, sir. How on earth did you know about Bird – that he was the bugger who'd kidnapped the lass?'

'Later, Bob, eh? When I'm more compos mentis. Just fill me in from your end.'

Bob could tell Snow was getting a little agitated so he dropped that particular query.

'A motorist found the girl wandering on the road in a distressed condition not far from the golf club cottage. Her hands were covered in blood and she was gibbering. Eventually this guy was able to get some sense out her, called the police and we found you and Bird up at the cottage. It was Bosworth who got there first. He said you both looked dead, lying there on the carpet. "Still as corpses you were", he said.' Bob smiled. 'Always was a bit of a drama queen, Bosworth.'

'Is Bird …?'

'Well, he's alive but …' Bob Fellows grimaced and wound his right hand in a circular motion up by the side of his head. 'Doolally, I'm afraid.'

'In what way?'

'It seems there is severe brain damage. That lass gave him a right going over. Mind you, can't blame her, the bastard deserved it. The docs have said he's now … what was the phrase … "in a vegetative state". As I said, doolally.'

Snow did not know how to react to this news. Feelings of relief and regret mingled in his still foggy mind.

'What about the little girl?'

'Ah, she's coming round. She's not exactly in a good place yet, but they reckon in time she'll make a full recovery. There's little physical damage but mentally she's still a bit spaced out. She has no memory of the attack which, I suppose, is a good thing. Something like that could really freak the lass out for the rest of her life. She was sedated at first but has been weaned off the drugs now. She's a gutsy little thing. She's been able to give us a statement of what she remembers, the kidnap and stuff – but that's all. We just need your version now – but that can wait, can't it, until you are up and about and your normal self.'

Snow nodded gently. 'I suppose so,' he said.

'Oh, I forgot,' cried Bob suddenly, wriggling in his chair. 'You've got an admirer.'

'Oh?'

'Well, as you can imagine this business has been in the papers. Well, that headmistress at Elizabeth's school seems most concerned about you. Came to the HQ to ask if you were all right, how you were going on etc. I reckon she fancies you. I saw the way she looked at you in her office …'

'What bloody nonsense. She'll just be relieved her pupil is safe.'

'Bloody nonsense yourself, sir. I know what I know and what I saw.' He winked at Snow in an exaggerated fashion.

Snow couldn't help himself but smile.

'When d'you reckon you'll be out of here?'

'By the weekend, but I've been told to take a week or so to recover fully.'

'Well, I'd take advantage of the break. There'll be a hell of a lot of paperwork waiting on your desk.'

'I can't wait.' And Snow meant it. He longed to be out of this hospital cocoon, away from the white walls, the smell of antiseptic and the hushed atmosphere, and back in the thick of it again, and if that meant writing reports and filling forms and other mundane tasks, so be it. He would welcome the tasks with open arms.

When Bob had gone, Snow sat propped up on his pillows, staring at the wall opposite, lost in thought. What on earth was he going to say about Bird in his statement? How could he explain his actions? What reasons could he come up with for breaking into the man's house and tracing him to the golf cottage? If Bird was, as Bob had averred, 'doolally', Snow realised that it provided an opportunity to massage the facts and avoid any mention of Bird's obsession with him and the implications that would bring. But what would he say? To be more precise: what lies would he construct?

With these troubled thoughts swimming around his brain, he drifted once more into the safe realm of sleep.

He was woken some time later by a nurse who held a mug of tea in her hand.

'You're a popular one today,' she said breezily, placing the mug in Snow's unsteady hand, the warmth bringing him a strange kind of comfort. 'You've another visitor. The second this afternoon.' She threw a glance towards a figure standing in the doorway. Snow focused his sleepy eyes on it. It was Matilda Shawcross, the head teacher of St Jude's.

'I hope you don't mind me popping in,' she said with an apprehensive smile. 'I've just been to see Elizabeth in another ward and I thought …'

'Hello.' Snow returned the smile. 'I'm very happy to see anyone from the outside world …' He paused awkwardly, realising that this sounded like a back-handed compliment. 'Please, come and sit down.'

She did so and the nurse bustled out of the room.

'How are you?'

'To be honest, I'm not sure. I've not been allowed out of bed yet.'

'It must have been quite an ordeal.'

'Actually, I can't remember much.'

'Well, it's thanks to you, Elizabeth is safe. You're a bit of a hero.'

'A colourful character at least,' he said, indicating his face. 'My sergeant thinks I look like a Picasso painting.'

She smiled. 'Oh, that's unkind but I must admit you are wearing quite a palette.'

'Thanks,' he said with mock gruffness and they both smiled and then lapsed into an awkward silence.

'You've just seen Elizabeth?' Snow said at length. 'How is she?'

'A little subdued, somewhat confused, but I think she's on the mend. Thankfully, she has blocked a lot of unpleasant detail from her mind.'

'That's good.'

'Mr Snow … er, Inspector …'

'Oh, please call me Paul. I feel a bit ridiculous being referred to as "inspector" wearing hospital pyjamas and a face like a road map.'

She smiled again and not for the first time Paul thought it was a lovely smile. Somehow it emphasised her elegance and intelligence, qualities that he always admired.

'OK, Paul. Do you like Indian food?'

For a fleeting moment, Snow was nonplussed by this sudden change of direction in the conversation. 'Indian food?' he repeated, unable to keep the puzzlement out of his voice. 'Well, yes.'

'I make a mean biryani with all the trimmings, naan bread and all. I was wondering, when you're back on your feet properly and your face has regained its normal colour, if you'd like to come round to my place and sample the delights of my curry.'

'You're inviting me to dinner?' Snow could not keep the surprise out of his voice.

'Brilliant deduction, Watson.' There was that smile again.

New territory was opening here and he was uncertain how he felt about it, but he found himself nodding. 'Well, that's very kind.'

'So … is that a date?'

'Well, yes, that's a date.'

THIRTY-TWO

Three days later Paul Snow was deemed fit to be released into the world again. He had undergone another brain scan and was told that everything was fine. His face was still showing the multi-coloured hues of severe bruising but he knew these would eventually fade, although his nose might bear a few scars. He was warned that he would most likely suffer from bad headaches for a couple of months, but apart from that, time would be the healer.

Before he left the hospital, he asked if he could see Colin Bird. There was a little reluctance by the doctor in charge of the case, but because of Snow's rank and involvement in the affair, he relented. Snow was taken to another part of the hospital and into a room similar to the one he had been staying in. Sitting in an upright chair by the bed with a hospital blanket over his knees was Colin Bird. He too had a face of many colours along with several gashes to his cheek and forehead. He stared with glassy, immobile eyes ahead of him, making no movement as Snow and the doctor entered.

'Hello, Colin, there's a visitor for you.'

There was no reaction.

The doctor moved over and took Bird's hand and squeezed it. Slowly, his head turned, but the features remained still and the eyes failed to register any emotion. Bird raised his gaze to take in Snow but there was no sign of recognition there at all.

Snow felt sick to his stomach. What had Bob Fellows said? Something about him being in a vegetative state. That was a polite way of indicating that he was dead from the neck up.

'There's no one at home, I'm afraid, and there's a real probability that there never will be,' said the doctor. 'When his wounds are healed, he'll be taken to a mental institution for tests, but I'm afraid for him it's a life spent with the shutters down.'

Snow nodded grimly and turned to the door. He had seen enough.

Some moments later he was stepping out of the hospital into the bright sunshine and facing the real world once more. The real, dark, complicated, dangerous and demanding world.

ABOUT THE AUTHOR

DAVID STUART DAVIES left teaching to become editor of *Sherlock Magazine* and is generally regarded as an expert on Sherlock Holmes, having written six novels, film books and plays featuring the character. He has given presentations on Holmes at many festivals and conferences as well as on board the *Queen Mary II*. He appeared as toastmaster at the Sherlock Holmes Dinner at Bloody Scotland in 2012 – Scotland's first international crime writing festival. He also created his own detective, wartime private eye Johnny Hawke, who has appeared in six novels. David is a member of the national committee of the Crime Writers' Association and has edited their monthly members' magazine, *Red Herrings*, since 1999. He has also been a Fellow of the Royal Literary Fund at Huddersfield University since 2012. He lives in Huddersfield, West Yorkshire.

Visit David's website at:

www.davidstuartdavies.co.uk

PRAISE FOR
DAVID STUART DAVIES

'David Stuart Davies knows how to write and how to twist the knife in the reader's mind.'

Peter James on *Innocent Blood*

'It's dark but delicious.'

Gyles Brandreth on *Brothers in Blood*

'I loved each chronicle, they were each very different and showed David Stuart Davies' talent for creating well-rounded characters in seven different situations. I felt I knew Luther Darke after just the first tale but still had more to learn. A great collection of short historical stories.'

Crime Book Club on *The Darke Chronicles*

'Charming, wistful and pleasingly nasty, as is only proper.'

Mark Gatiss on *The Halloween Mask*

'One of the best Holmes pastiches of all.'

Crime Time on *The Tangled Skein*

'I just can't keep quiet about this book. It is a real page turner, an exhilarating roller coast ride of suspense, appalling crimes, hidden clues, with more twists and turns than a dark foreboding maze. Come! Join the chase ... after all the game is afoot!'

Mystery Net Community on *The Veiled Detective*

'A thundering good yarn ... I wholeheartedly recommend it to anyone who has an affection for Holmes and a good, old-fashioned page turner.'

Sleuthing the Shelves on *The Scroll of the Dead*

The first Detective Inspector Paul Snow novel

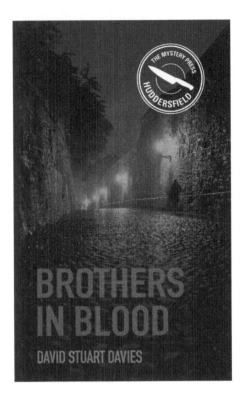

A brutal game devised by three intelligent but bored teenagers escalates into murder. Led by the charismatic and cunning Laurence, the trio of 'brothers' meets once a year to carry out untraceable, motiveless murders – for fun. Until, years later, they must murder in order to protect one of their own, leaving themselves vulnerable to discovery. This killing is investigated by Detective Inspector Paul Snow, a complex man with a secret of his own which links him to the murder. As Snow grows closer to unmasking the killers, his professional life begins to unravel in a terrifying fashion.

Find this title and more at
www.thehistorypress.co.uk

Also from The History Press

We are proud to present our historical crime fiction imprint, The Mystery Press, featuring a dynamic and growing list of titles written by diverse and respected authors, united by the distinctiveness and excellence of their writing. From a collection of thrilling tales by the CWA Short Story Dagger award-winning Murder Squad, to a Victorian lady detective determined to solve some sinister cases of murder in London, these books will appeal to serious crime fiction enthusiasts as well as those who simply fancy a rousing read.

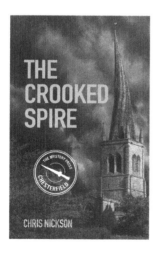

Find these titles and more at
www.thehistorypress.co.uk

Lightning Source UK Ltd.
Milton Keynes UK
UKOW07f0945211114

241969UK00002B/3/P